MW00974189

tutored

tutored

ALLISON WHITTENBERG

DELACORTE PRESS

This is a work of fiction. Names, characters, places, and incidents either are the product of the author's imagination or are used fictitiously. Any resemblance to actual persons, living or dead, events, or locales is entirely coincidental.

Copyright © 2010 by Allison Whittenberg

All rights reserved. Published in the United States by Delacorte Press, an imprint of Random House Children's Books, a division of Random House, Inc., New York.

Delacorte Press is a registered trademark and the colophon is a trademark of Random House, Inc.

Visit us on the Web! www.randomhouse.com/teens
Educators and librarians, for a variety of teaching tools,
visit us at www.randomhouse.com/teachers

Library of Congress Cataloging-in-Publication Data
Whittenberg, Allison.
Tutored / by Allison Whittenberg. — 1st ed.
p. cm.
Summary: In Philadelphia, two African American teenagers from different backgrounds become romantically close when one tutors the other.
ISBN 978-0-385-73869-9 (alk. paper)—ISBN 978-0-385-90742-2 (lib. bdg.)—ISBN 978-0-375-89577-7 (ebook)
1. African Americans—Pennsylvania—Philadelphia—Juvenile fiction.
[1. African Americans—Fiction. 2. Prejudices—Fiction. 3. Tutors and tutoring—Fiction. 4. Philadelphia (Pa.)—Fiction.] I. Title.
PZ7.W6179Tu 2010   [Fic]—dc22   2009041641

The text of this book is set in 11.5-point Dutch 801 Roman.
Book design by Vikki Sheatsley
Printed in the United States of America
10 9 8 7 6 5 4 3 2 1
First Edition

Random House Children's Books supports the First Amendment and celebrates the right to read.

Acknowledgments

I want to thank:

Super Senior Editor Stephanie Lane Elliott for lending her expertise once again. It's been great working with you over the years.

Wonderful agent Sara Crowe, who is always so supportive and insightful.

Mystery writer Jonathan Maberry for his referral. It's nice when one artist concerns himself with another artist's career.

Early readers of my work: Lynn Watts, Stacy Goldberger, Kathleen Butts, and Minna Hong—oh, what I put you through.

Poet Lamont Steptoe (Philly's own Walt Whitman) for being so accessible.

Kristine Grow, Margaret Kenton, Barbara Torode, Mike Cohen, Steve Delia, Lynne Campbell, John Sevcik, and Mel Brake for all your suggestions, support, and friendship.

My main man, Marlowe, who made writing this book extra special.

tutored

1

Are you a minority? Unemployed, underemployed, or economically disadvantaged? We serve the entire West Side, and we have services that can assist you to a new FUTURE! Stop by today.

Hakiam read this pasteup at least half a dozen times before he decided that it was time to turn to the wall and start like you mean to finish. Still, he was frowning as he approached the converted row houses, four stories high, spliced into sections for businesses and nonprofits. He entered the east wing.

Inside, there were pamphlets on the table and posters on every wall promising cures for social problems. One poster read, "Build, Brother, build!" and featured a few dark-skinned individuals looking cheerful. Though not a living soul was around, he felt like someone was pointing at him. All this paraphernalia felt aimed at him, like a cannon.

An arrow on the wall told him that the study center

was on the second floor, and to get to it one had to climb an enormous spiral staircase. Right there, that was enough to turn anyone in his or her right mind away. But he decided to go up. As he mounted the steps, Hakiam heard a female voice, and upon reaching the top of the stairs, he followed it. He pressed on to see some circular tables and a couple of bookshelves housing a small lending library off to the right. At the far end of the room, behind a big desk, standing with her back to him, was a young woman. Like him, she was black. He had seen her type before. She was all dressed up in a willow-green roll-neck sweater, a long skirt with microdots, and low leather boots. She was cradling a telephone receiver under her chin as if it were a violin.

She turned around as he approached her and beamed at him. She quickly rid herself of the person on the other end of the line with a hasty "I will keep a sharp lookout for that shipment. Thank you so much for the donation." Then she hung up the phone.

"You work here?" he asked.

Her smile faded. "No, I'm just pretending," she said in a voice thick with sarcasm.

When she stepped out from behind the desk, he got a better view of her and her small-boned features. He concluded that she was way too thin and big-eyed. "It was just a damn question. You ain't got to get all uppity," he replied.

"You're right. I apologize." She wasn't one to hold grudges, it seemed, because her smile quickly returned. "Please, have a seat. Can I get you some tea or juice?" He noticed how she spoke very soft and fine, taking the time to pronounce every syllable. Right then, he decided he really didn't like her. She seemed like she'd stepped out of some corny, boring old movie.

Wendy sensed the boy's judgment and also found herself giving him the once-over. He had chiseled features: cheekbones that asserted themselves and eyes that slanted at the outer corners. His mouth curved in a surly way and he had a dead look in his eyes. She continued to scan his frame and wondered why, since he had a nice build, he couldn't find any clothing in his size. Both his pants and his shirt fit like he'd borrowed them from a gigantically tall, morbidly obese neighbor. She knew that was the style, but if she'd been a guy with a decent physique, she was sure she would have wanted to show the world and not walk around in tent gear.

She rearranged her smile. "Welcome to the center."

"Are you a tutor or just a secretary?" he asked her.

"I'm a tutor."

"In what?" he quizzed her.

"Any subject you'd like. I'd be happy to help you." She offered her hand.

He just glared at it.

"I'm not contagious," she told him, gesturing to the seat again.

He shook his head. "Look, I hope this won't take long. I just wanted to sign up."

"Are you in some kind of hurry?" she asked.

"No, I just don't want to waste time."

3

"I won't waste your time or mine," she said. "Please, have a seat while I look over your paperwork."

This time he sat, but he told her he didn't have any paperwork.

"Well, how could that be? Didn't you sign in downstairs?"

"Ain't nobody down there."

She got up and went to the top of the stairs. "Mr. Clayton. Mr. Clayton," she called. Her words echoed unanswered in the cavernous room.

"I don't know where he went," she told Hakiam as she walked back. "He's supposed to be there to orient people when they come in."

"Well, it doesn't look like there's any mad rush on the place."

"How did you get in if he wasn't there to buzz you in?"

"The door was open."

Wendy got up and peered out the window. She looked right, then left, only to spot the receptionist about a block away, crossing the street, holding a white Styrofoam box.

"Don't worry," Hakiam continued. "You don't have shit worth stealing in here. All you have is books."

She counted to ten in her head, not wanting to show her annoyance, then pulled out a blank form from the desk and asked for his name. When he said Hakiam Powell, she asked him to spell it.

"They didn't teach you how to spell where you come from?"

"I'll sound it out," she told him. "Age?"

"Where are you from?" he asked.

4

"What difference does that make to you?"

He didn't answer.

"How old are you?" she asked again.

"Seventeen."

"You're young enough to go to a regular high school; why would you take equivalency classes?"

"I missed too much of regular school to go back."

"How far did you get?"

He just smirked.

Her eyes narrowed. "Is this the way it's going to go? You dance around every other question?"

He gave her an even more defiant smirk.

Just then, she heard the door open downstairs, and then Mr. Clayton's voice: "Hey, Wendy, you want some of my wings?"

"No," Wendy yelled back, turning her attention back to Hakiam. "Do you know you have to be at least eighteen to enroll in this program?"

"Then put down that I'm twenty-five."

She frowned. "You look twenty-five like I look twenty-five."

He leaned in close to her. "You do look twenty-five. Or thirty."

There was a pause while she absorbed his barb, and he let out a chuckle.

"Well, if you are so inspired, I won't tell on you." She wrote the lie down on the form.

"Address?" she asked.

After he ran that down, he asked, "Want to swing by tonight? I could really show you some things."

5

She tightened her already tight expression and told him, "No thanks. I'm busy."

She went over to the copier and made him a duplicate. Then she pulled out a three-ring binder and made some markings in it. "Classes are held Monday through Thursday. Roll call is taken. You miss three sessions, you are out of the program. Any questions?"

"Yeah, why do you talk like you're white?" he asked, and waited for her to flinch.

She didn't.

"Do you have any questions *about the program*?"

He rose from the chair and grinned. "Yeah, how come you didn't offer me any wings?"

2

Actually, Wendy really wasn't that busy tonight, unless you counted reclining on the sofa with her legs curled up watching the evening news as a frenzy of activity. She had changed into a sweatshirt and shorts, and opted for the network fare—cable had too many pop-ups and streaming headlines.

Still, the half-hour nightly news had really gotten predictable. A little about the war, a little about gas prices, a little about the stock market, something about one of the cancers (breast or colon, usually), and a cutesy human-interest story at the very end to prove life really wasn't so bad. Tonight, it was about a bear that had wandered into a swimming pool, charming all in the area. Wendy had nothing against bears, but after hearing all that doom and gloom, she found it hard to switch gears to an "animals do the darnedest things" story.

By her side was her mail from that day; she opened it as she spooned hot broccoli-and-cheddar soup into her mouth. Every piece was from a college admissions officer. Those were the only people who knew she was alive. She heard from ten a day, at least. Some envelopes were thick (those contained catalogs), others were thin (those were invitations to open houses). Each was enticing. Colleges really knew how to put their best face forward—and what faces, so happy and blemish-free! (Were those really members of the student body or were they professional models?)

She was a junior and knew she had to make her decision soon, but she was hesitating. It wasn't that she didn't want to continue her studies after high school. It was just that all the colleges that approached her seemed so safe and mainstream. She wanted an adventure! She would love to forgo the whole idea of college and just do independent study. Homeschooling seemed to be in, with homeschooled kids cleaning up at spelling bees and science fairs. Maybe she could start a new trend, home-collegeing—work a deal with the state, show proof of her progress, and at the end, voilà, she could have her BA without all the BS.

Turning back to the TV, she watched the bear splash about in the blue water, thinking her dad would throw a natural fit if she didn't go to a traditional college. As an accountant, Mr. Anderson was so proud of his own advanced education. Something like that (practical, steady) was what he really wanted for Wendy. He wanted her to have her life set. Sometimes when they argued, Wendy wished she still had the buffer of her mother. Her mother could make her dad back off. There were at least a billion reasons why Wendy longed for her mother to still be alive; that was just one of them.

As she broke off a piece of crusty bread from the bakery, her dad made his way to the club chair holding a steaming bowl in one hand and *Time* magazine in the other. He never changed after work, aside from taking off his overcoat. He seemed comfortable in his pressed trousers, starched shirt, and blue sweater vest.

He located the remote control and switched the channel to CNN without asking her. Without glancing her way, he asked, "So, how are things in the ghetto?"

3

Hakiam kept his eyes front, jaw clenched, and shoulders hunched as he made his way down Lancaster Avenue. He was thirsty, but every bodega he passed had the same posting in the window: *No more than two students allowed in at one time*. Since it was after three, the owners were busy fussing from the door at their youthful would-be patrons and/or thieves. An already clustering group was yelling back in protest. Hakiam kept his distance, frowning. What were these owners trying to say? "No one else lifts things, just students"? Hakiam never seriously considered breaking the rule by going in; who wanted that much hassle over a Coke? He kept his hands in his pockets and kept making strides.

Next, he passed a Laundromat, a rank rib restaurant, and a wig shop. Strewn about the sidewalk was broken glass from soft-drink and beer bottles as well as car break-ins. At least the shards weren't airborne, like the candy and fast-food wrappers that blew across the asphalt streets.

A homeless man passed Hakiam, regarding him with bloodshot eyes of complete resignation. He was ragged and dirty, with a soiled, unbuttoned shirt, and pants that looked five million years old. His hair was also rough, as if it hadn't felt a comb, ever. Hakiam followed the man a bit with his eyes. He felt sorry for the homeless who were stranded in the hood. They were totally gone, bereft of even the wherewithal to panhandle properly like the homeless in Center City. He imagined the vast emptiness of their lives, with not even a corner to claim, where they could ask for a quarter for a cup of coffee. How low.

Hakiam passed another rib shack. This time the air smelled sweet. He liked spare ribs; his aunt used to fix them when he lived with her. He and his play brother used to polish off so many they'd lose count. A platter and some fruit punch would go great together, but he only had a five on him—not enough for all that. And besides, he was in a hurry. He had to meet his cousin Leesa and pick up her baby.

He turned up Forty-first Street and entered the social services center.

Inside there was life, and plenty of it. He scanned the array of hairstyles in hopes of locating Leesa's no-drama close crop. He looked past the kinky twists, the butt-length braids, and the good old-fashioned perms, searching and searching.

"Did you sign in?" the intake worker behind the long desk asked him.

Hakiam eyed the desk. All the counselors wore scrubs in various pastels. He couldn't tell which one had spoken to him.

"I'm just here to find someone," he said to all six of them. This was the fifth time he'd been here. This was where Leesa (a mother, ten weeks in) picked up her bi-weekly checks, along with her vouchers for formula, eggs, milk, and cheese (American cheese, of course, not provolone or mozzarella—those were too fancy to be covered).

In this place, some women were pregnant, some weren't but had kids with them, and some had kids on both the inside and the outside. One girl with a protruding stomach had four children gathered around her. When Hakiam finally zeroed in on his cousin, he also spotted her quivering baby, Malikia. Hakiam hoped that she'd get that pudgy Gerber look any day now, but he wouldn't bet money on it. Malikia had been fifteen weeks premature, so technically she shouldn't have even been seen by human eyes yet.

"How long you been here?" he asked Leesa.

She shrugged.

"Are you next?" he asked her.

She shrugged again.

As Leesa moved her shoulders up and down, Hakiam couldn't help but look at his cousin's asymmetrical breasts. On each was tattooed a rose. He wondered why she would get tatoos that accentuated the lopsidedness of her body. Of course, she had others. She had names, pictures, and phrases, in blue and red ink on the dark brown skin of her upper arms and shins. She had an eagle above her butt crack. Hakiam had seen all this in the short time he'd been bunking at her place; Leesa would never get an award for modesty.

The room was stuffy. No air circulating because (for security reasons) none of the windows were open. The staleness heightened the agitation of some of the mommies. They repeatedly told their kids to "Sit sit sit" like it was a dog-training school. But that was miles better than "Quit crying or I'll give you something to cry about."

Kids were grabbed and shoved. The women at the front desk didn't seem to be making note of it, though, and if they weren't going to say anything, Hakiam sure as hell wasn't.

Keep your eyes front.

"Is there a water fountain in here?" Hakiam asked.

Leesa gestured to the wall and Hakiam walked over to the fountain there. The pressure was low. There was no gush, just a trickle. He sucked in as much as he could; then he heard Leesa's name called.

He met up with her and the baby by the counter. Leesa spread several forms and documents out on the desk. The intake worker paged through the pile and said, "State or federal ID?"

"I'm looking for it," Leesa said.

The woman finally looked up to see Leesa still rooting through her bag while hoisting Malikia onto her shoulder.

"You came without ID?" the woman asked.

"Shit," Leesa said.

The intake worker pointed to a sign. "What does that say?"

Hakiam read aloud, "'Federal or state ID is required.'"

The woman threw a glare at him. "What's your name?"

"Hakiam."

She checked the sheet. "You're not listed."

"I know I ain't," Hakiam said. "I'm just with her."

The woman shook her head. "You have to be on the sheet."

"Look, I have everything else," Leesa said. Malikia began slipping and Leesa gave her another boost.

"I'm not losing my job over you. You need to have everything," the woman said.

"No one's asking you to lose your job," Leesa told her.

"Well then, come back when you have everything."

Hakiam saw his cousin lunge for the woman and he reached out to brace her arm. "Just forget it," he said.

"I ain't forgetting nothing," Leesa said, stepping up her voice. "Who do you think you are, lady? Can't you see I got a goddamn baby here—"

At that point, Hakiam really got hold of her. He ushered her toward the door. "Why didn't you inventory your stuff before you were called by the caseworker?"

"What am I supposed to be, perfect? Do you know how many things I have to think of? Malikia was wailing her head off before you came—"

14

Hakiam blocked out the rest of what she was saying. This was her way. She was a crisis frog; she hopped from one lily pad of trouble to the next. She was never prepared.

Hakiam glanced back at the packed waiting area. There were paternity handouts on a side desk. "Every Child Has the Right to Know Who His Legal Father Is," one pamphlet's cover read.

"It's nearly time for me to be at work. It'll be next month before I get another appointment. Shit. Do you know how much time I've wasted here just to end up with jack?" Leesa asked him.

Hakiam didn't answer her; he was too busy eavesdropping on a client being asked by a caseworker, "Are you registered to vote?"

Back on the outside, a group of boys were going at each other. Hakiam couldn't tell if they were playing or not. In the navy blue tie and slacks and crisp shirt of his school uniform, the one in the center was being smacked in the face. The other four were hitting him this way and that.

The group moved and Hakiam stepped out to block any blow to the baby as she was handed off to him.

Leesa asked him for his bus pass.

"I don't have one. I walked here."

"Didn't they give you a bus pass at the GED place?"

Hakiam shook his head.

"Did they at least give you tokens?"

"Nope."

"Everybody else I know got at least that from them.

15

Make sure you get what you're supposed to get," she told him.

Leesa booked it to the corner to catch the number 21 bus downtown.

"I'll be home the usual time," she said before she left them. She raised a hand to wave goodbye, more to him than to her baby.

Hakiam stood there for a moment, the eight-and-a-half-pound infant twitching in his arms. It was clear now that those kids were in the thick of a beat-down. Another vagrant went by in yellow-stained jeans, rolling a shopping cart filled with tin cans and scrap metal. Hakiam thought for a moment about why he had moved in with his cousin. His fresh start was quickly turning to an SOS (same old shit), and God was he ever thirsty.

4

he ghetto. Wendy's father's comment was typical of him. His favorite saying was "I help poor people all the time—by not being one." He was very proud of the fact that he had yanked himself up by the proverbial bootstraps, and he wanted the world to know it. Though he was raised in one of the don't be there sections of the city, he had been able to not only stay out of trouble with the law (not so much as a parking ticket) but also go to college (Indiana University of Pennsylvania on a one-thousand-dollar minority scholarship; the rest he made up with work-study and loans) and become gainfully employed (bringing home the high end of five figures yearly).

Wendy knew it was one of her father's goals in life not to look back, and certainly not to give back. She was just the opposite, which usually put them at odds. Like last term, when Wendy was involved with a volunteer organization that cleaned and painted inner-city schools. Her father had insisted on picking her up after these sessions, although it would have been fine with her to ride public transportation.

One day when they'd swung by Tannery Duckery Elementary School on Diamond Street, he had surprised her by suggesting they grab a bite to eat.

"You want to eat out here?" Wendy asked. "You must be starving."

"I am."

He decided on a Broad Street eatery that was on the cusp: the Temple University students in one direction, neighborhood people in the other.

"This looks decent," he said.

Wendy's father ordered a strawberry malt and a quarter-pound burger cooked rare with guacamole, jalapeño jack, and pico de gallo. Wendy ordered a mini-hamburger, well done, and a cherry Coke.

They sat near the front and were just starting to make small talk about the weather when a ruckus started.

From where Wendy was sitting with her back to the counter, she heard raised voices and turned to see what was going on. A man who looked about her dad's age was arguing with the restaurant's manager.

"I saw you fill it up with soda. Water is clear."

"No it ain't, sucker."

"That' s stealing. I saw you."

"You think that just because a black man comes up in here he's looking for trouble."

The other man spoke in a calmer, more even tone. "You don't have to bring race into this."

"Race *been* in this, you goddamn cracker!" he roared.

"Calm down, please."

"I hate stupid crackers like you."

"That man is certainly loud enough," Wendy's dad said.

"Dad, *shhh,*" Wendy told him with a here-we-go roll of her eyes. The last thing she needed was for her dad to get into this scuffle.

"He could pay for his drink like everyone else," her dad told her.

Wendy was watching the rest of the patrons. She marveled at how this man had single-handedly changed the mood of the entire restaurant.

Two people had pulled out their cell phones and started recording. Everyone watched in complete silence, not moving a muscle. If the accused soda thief was looking for hand-to-hand combat, he would have done something by now, Wendy figured. He also had no buddies with him; he would have called them for backup. Still, all seemed whipped into a near panic by this guy who wanted a free soda. What was everyone afraid of?

Wendy eyed a man with a strawberry sundae whose forehead was tense with alarm. Then she turned to watch another woman, who was hastily packing up her belongings. The woman slipped out the door, leaving a half-finished turkey club behind.

All at once, the man at the center of everything left, and there was a collective sigh of relief. People went back to enjoying their meals.

Then it started again.

Wendy saw a little boy's eyes widen. "Ma, he's back," he told his mother.

Someone asked, "What's he want now?"

Wendy turned around.

"Listen, you goddamn racist, I want to speak to the manager!" the man shouted.

"I am the manager."

"That figures, you old racist goddamn cracker!"

"I'm going to call the police in five seconds."

"I am not going to let you push me around, don't tell me that a nigger can't get no water when he wants some water."

"Please leave."

"I'm gonna kick your ass."

"Please leave."

"I should have known that we shouldn't come here," Wendy's dad mumbled.

Just then the irate man began taking his message straight to the people.

He eyed Wendy's dad and zeroed in.

"You with me, brother?" he asked Wendy's father, as if he was already assured of the affirmative answer.

Wendy's dad straightened his shoulders, looked him dead in the eye, and enunciated two words: "Hell, no."

The man stepped back. "Oh, so it's like that, Uncle Tom?"

"You must be out of your mind to think that I would take part in this foolishness in the presence of my daughter. If that makes me an Uncle Tom, then I'll be one gladly."

Now Wendy's heart pounded. She had no idea what was going to happen next. Would the man take his anger out on her father? Would her father be dumb enough to incense him further?

She never found out. Before the man had a chance to react, the police burst into the restaurant and hauled him away.

During the ride home, Wendy had had to listen on and on about how "this" was "proof."

"And you wonder why we live in the suburbs?" Wendy's dad asked. "That was exhibit A right there."

"Dad, one bad apple doesn't spoil the whole bunch."

Her dad laughed at that as he turned onto the highway. "Where I grew up, I had to deal with poor excuses for human beings like that all the time."

"Maybe he really didn't have the money for a soda, Dad."

"Then he shouldn't have a soda. There's no need to terrorize a restaurant like that."

"*Terrorize?*" Wendy asked. "Don't you think that's a little strong? He's not Osama bin Laden."

"Don't make excuses for that idiot. And remind me to never let myself get hungry in the slums."

"Dad, something like that could happen anywhere."

"Oh, sure, Wendy, sure."

"It could."

Wendy's father switched to cruise control.

"I don't want to hear it, Wendy. All your life I have tried to keep you in a nice, quiet, safe place, but you seem hell-bent on putting yourself in harm's way. We could have been shot!"

"He didn't even have a gun. All he did was talk. How could we have been shot?"

"Well, *he* could have been. When we get home to Bryn Mawr, I am going to kiss the ground."

Ever since that afternoon, Mr. Anderson had amped up his tirades against "those areas" and "those people." This was of course the main reason Wendy sought out more opportunities to volunteer. Now that Wendy was working at the center, with a whole new group of so-called hoodlums, she and her dad were fighting more than ever.

5

There were GED classes back in Cincinnati, but Hakiam had wanted a fresh start. He was totally burned out on Ohio. He knew every back alley. Every one-way street. Every dead end. It was time for a change. The day he decided to leave, he had just finished serving a juvie sentence for shoplifting. That day his counselor, a tweed-blazer-patch-on-the elbow-professor-looking-with-the-bright-yellow-shiny-happy-button-down-shirt-wearing, underfed forty-something white man, signed him out.

"What are your plans now, Hakiam?" the counselor had asked.

"Philadelphia."

"Who do you know there?"

"A cousin and an aunt. They used to live here but then she got divorced. My aunt did."

"So you know her pretty well?"

"Five years ago I did. They used to live two blocks away from my old house."

"Do you have a job lined up? Are you going to finish your education? Enroll in a high school there?"

"Yep," Hakiam had said by reflex. He knew it was what the counselor wanted to hear.

The man handed Hakiam the paperwork he needed.

"I'm done?" Hakiam asked, just to make sure.

The man nodded and Hakiam took his folding chair to the wall.

"Just one more thing," the counselor said, holding up his pointer finger for emphasis. "Remember: an open palm gets more than a closed fist."

Hakiam had almost busted out laughing. What kind of advice was that to send someone off to start a new life with? That was a formula for disaster. In Hakiam's experience, the few times he'd chosen to be nice and trusting he'd gotten stepped on and crushed.

Hakiam wanted a new life. He never wanted to return to the one that he'd had.

At the end of the week, he paid seventy-five dollars to Greyhound and boarded a bus headed east.

He started feeling low immediately.

All around him, he saw failure. As each passenger climbed aboard, emptiness filled the bus. Hakiam saw the unshaven and the unshowered. The angry and confused dragging their duffel bags. Beside him, an old man took out his plastic-wrapped sandwiches.

Hakiam stared out the windows like a peeping Tom. Riding the bus never meant passing City Hall or going by the nice restaurants or boutiques. There were no businessmen with wedding bands checking briefcases, no friendly pedestrians strolling past. No, instead he saw a squeegee man dirtying clean windshields.

Many hours later, he was in Philadelphia.

6

While cleaning up after dinner, Wendy gave her best friend, Erin, a call. She wedged the phone between her ear and shoulder as she placed her cup, small dish, and spoon in the dishwasher.

"So what happened at the center today?" Erin asked. She was still at the skating rink where she worked. Wendy could hear the eighties rock in the background.

"Nothing much, it was really slow. There was a new guy who came in. I don't know how long he's going to last."

"Hey, aren't people who work with the disenfranchised supposed to be optimistic?"

"Yeah, but I can tell. When I see someone roll in coppin' a 'tude—"

"Talk that talk, sister," Erin interrupted.

"You mean 'sista,'" Wendy corrected.

"Sorry, I flunked Ebonics in middle school," Erin said.

"Don't let that hold you back. There's a tutorial every night on *Sucker Free*."

"Whoa!"

"I don't mean to be cynical, but the dude seemed really immature and snarling and arrogant and insulting and weird—"

"So when are you two going on your first date?"

"That'll be the day. I hate people like him."

"How bad can he be? If he made his way in there, he must want help. He must want to 'improve his station in life,' as they say."

"Erin, why aren't you interning at the center instead of me? You seem like the one who drank the Kool-Aid."

"What's Kool-Aid have to do with anything?"

"Jim Jones," Wendy said. "You know, that cult leader who took all his followers to Guyana and got them all to drink Kool-Aid."

"What's so bad about that?"

"It was poisoned."

"I don't follow, Wendy."

"I'm not going to allow myself to be brainwashed. I've been at the center for two weeks—"

"Well, that's a lifetime."

"I'm not a true believer, Erin, I never was. It's just as insulting to excuse away bad behavior from a person just because he comes from the streets—"

"That's right! It's *their* fault. Who makes the streets the streets anyway? It's the people who live there," her father shouted from the next room.

It frosted her when her father eavesdropped. "This isn't on three-way, Dad."

"What did he say?" Erin asked.

"Never mind," Wendy said, "he's taking me off point. All I'm saying is that if you come into a new environment, why do you have to have a chip on your shoulder? Why do you—"

"Tell Erin I said hello," her father said.

"Okay, Dad," Wendy told him. "Erin, he says hello."

"Oh, tell him I said hello," Erin said.

"This is not a three-way call!" Wendy said.

"Boy, you are strung out, Wendy. Maybe you need a vacation from volunteering."

"I like the center fine most days. I just don't like dealing with everybody's attitude."

"So what's his name, Wendy?"

"Hakiam. And you wouldn't find me going out with him. If he were the last man on earth, I'd date a tree first."

7

Whoever thought up the saying "sleeping like a baby" had lied. As far as Hakiam could tell, babies rarely slept. Here it was, after midnight, and Malikia was squirming and whimpering and whimpering and squirming. She showed no sign of letting up.

Hakiam decided to take her out to the fire escape, thinking the night air would soothe her. The air was warm, but the noise started almost immediately. A dog barked. Footsteps echoed from the sidewalks and bounced up the stairs. Someone started arguing about someone running off with their shit. Next came a steady stream of "your mother this" and "your mother that."

Malikia cried a tearless cry like the world was coming to an end. Hakiam was inclined to agree, but instead of weeping he took out a blunt. Smoking did two things for him. One, it cleared his mind, and two, it gave him something to do with his other hand. So he jiggled tiny, wrinkled Malikia and blew smoke into the blue-black night sky. His mind drifted to more pleasant thoughts, like how good the bed would feel when he finally got to it and could close his eyes.

He was still thirsty, though; Leesa had no juice or milk in the house. Soda was all she had, which anyone could tell you just made you thirstier the more you drank. He'd had three cans of Pepsi since he'd been back from social services.

As late as it was, he knew he wasn't going to get to look over his books for those GED classes. He wondered what that girl would say. What was her name? He hated that voice she used, like she was auditioning for a Shakespeare play. Why couldn't she just make it plain?

This would drive him crazy: what was that big-eyed girl's name? Sure, she annoyed him, but in his two months in this city of so-called brotherly love, she was the only candy striper he'd met. Was it Janet? Betty? How could he forget it so quickly after the run-in he'd had with her? For a second or two, he felt bad about the way he'd treated her.

After another blunt, the baby finally went down, and his mind then turned to how glad he was to be under the covers. He didn't give what's-her-name another thought.

8

"Keep a positive outlook and positive things will happen to you." That quotation was the heading in Wendy's daily planner. She tried this mind-over-matter approach as she sat in the center awaiting a client. She was wearing a raspberry V-neck T-shirt and a crinkly mahogany-colored rayon skirt. Her delicate features were arranged in an expression that was far from a smile but also far from a scowl.

And then he came in.

As he approached her, he held out a piece of paper. "Sign that to say I was here," he told her.

She up-and-downed him without expression. "Pardon?" she asked.

"Sign—"

"I heard you."

"Well?" he asked.

She peered at the sheet, then turned her head. She

31

reached into her bulging canvas bag and pulled out a thick textbook.

"You can do that on your own time," he told her.

She further ignored him by opening her book to chapter nine and reading silently, occasionally marking a passage with her yellow highlighter.

He observed her for a while, sighing and resting his weight on alternating sides of his body, hoping she would react to his impatience. Finally he said, "I never took you for a goldbricker."

That made her look up. "What did you call me?"

"A goldbricker. You're goldbricking."

"And that means?"

"You're supposed to be tutoring people. . . ."

She placed her highlighter down and pushed her book to the side. "Exactly. I'm *supposed* to be *tutoring people*, but *people* haven't been coming in here to be *tutored*."

He frowned. "I'm here, ain't I?"

"You just want your paper signed. I'm on to you."

Hakiam took the seat beside her. "Look, you. I—"

"You? You mean to tell me you don't even know my name? Give me that paper."

When he did, she wrote quickly on it and handed it back to him.

He crumpled it up. "Look, how dumb do you think I am? I know you're not Paris Hilton."

Wendy laughed extra-loud just to needle him.

"I don't have time for this mess. I've been up all night."

She held her hand up to halt his talking. "One word, Hakiam: priorities."

"Whatever that means."

"It means if you want to waste your time hanging out with the homies—"

"Homies?" he asked, reeling at her dated slang. "Listen, you, I was watching a baby last night."

Her thin eyebrows arched. "A baby?"

"Yeah."

"A baby baby?" she asked.

He nodded.

"You have a baby. You didn't tell me that last time."

"It ain't mine."

Wendy took the cap off her highlighter and went back to reading her book. "You ought to get on *The Maury Povich Show*."

Hakiam grabbed her hand. Not wanting him to touch her, Wendy jerked back.

"Listen," he said. "It's my cousin's little girl. She's not even supposed to be here yet. She was born early and my cousin works nights at the late-night window and she said I could live there for free if I just watch her every now and then."

Wendy rolled her eyes. "What a setup. What's the little girl's name?"

"What difference does it make?"

"Everybody has a right to be called by a name, don't they? Even I have one, not that you bothered to remember."

"Look, that baby kept me up half the night with her wailing. I had to light up—"

Wendy slammed the book shut. "You smoked marijuana in front of an infant?"

"I didn't hear her complain."

"Secondhand smoke around a baby is very dangerous. It could lead to respiratory problems—"

He rolled his eyes and repeated, "Respiratory problems."

"Oh, so now you think asthma is funny?"

"I think asthma is hilarious."

"That's a very ignorant thing to say."

"Well, maybe I'm a very ignorant person," he said.

"And proud to be so. Besides contaminating the lungs of a premature infant, your own cognitive ability was compromised. What if an emergency happened and you had to react quickly? And where was her mother during all this?"

"I already told you. She was at work at the late-night window."

"What's her name, Hakiam?"

"Why do you got to know everyone's name? What difference does it make?"

"Don't brush this off. You have to be very careful when a baby is in your care."

"You know this ain't my kid, right? You're getting all worked up over nothing."

"Nothing? *Nothing?* You don't even know what nothing is. You said she was born early—how early?"

"I don't know. Couple weeks. A few months. I forget."

Wendy shook her head. "There's a big difference between weeks and months. The normal gestation period—"

"What is this, sex ed?"

"I'm just making you aware that in an infant the lungs are the last organs to develop—"

Hakiam spoke over her. "She ain't no more fragile than anyone else."

"Are you just trying to argue with me or are you totally insane?"

"I ain't come here for this shit. I'm here to be tutored in English and math and all I get is static from you. I'm trying to finish this thing and you have to be a bitch about everything and stand in my way."

Wendy packed up her belongings, rose from her seat, and slung her bag over her shoulder. She looked him right in the eye and told him, "Drop dead."

She was almost to the foot of the stairs when he recovered from her remark. He asked, "Hey, where are you going? Your sign says you're here until five p.m."

Wendy spun around, pointed her index finger at him, and said, "You better pray that nothing happens to that little baby, because if it does, I will make sure you get life in prison."

She turned around again and escaped from his sight.

He called after her, "Make up your mind, which one do you want? Do you want me to get life or drop dead?"

9

At six that evening, Hakiam's eyelids felt raw again. He reached his cousin's place about that time. It was Leesa's evening off from her job, so he hoped to get a full night's rest and let Leesa do diaper duty.

He came across her asleep, curled up like the baby by her side on the mattress. He frowned. Leesa had told him to always put Malikia in the crib. It had something to do with the fact that an adult's body could easily roll over and crush an infant. That was the lecture Leesa had given him, but, like most people he'd met, she had a different set of rules for herself.

His eyes swept to Malikia. She had her tiny hands balled up into tight fists, like she could handle herself.

He went into the other room and rooted through the fridge, only to be disappointed. It was a near-empty cavern containing just a few bottles of soda and half a stick of butter. No juice, no dairy products, no meat thawing, and no fruit. No eggs to fry up. Not even a slice of bread to toast. He slammed the refrigerator door and damned those voucher people.

What a household, he thought. Of all the places he'd been bounced to throughout his life, this took the cake (if only there were a cake to take).

Now he was wishing Leesa could have gotten the free-food voucher from social services. If she'd had the right ID, he could have made a meal of something. He couldn't wait till she rescheduled; he wanted something now.

Then he saw that on the kitchen table under her bag, there was a Styrofoam box with *B & FF* written on it in red marker. He opened it to find a hamburger, half eaten, and some french fries sopping with grease and ketchup. He pulled up a seat and chowed down on what was left of the meal, picking up on biting where Leesa had left off.

"Hakiam, what are you doing eating up my food?" Leesa said to him as she entered the room with Malikia stationed on her hip.

Luckily, Hakiam had eaten fast and was on his last bite. "I got to eat something, don't I?" he asked. "You ain't got nothing in the fridge. Nothing at all. What if Malikia needed some milk?"

"Babies can't drink cow's milk, doofus," Leesa told him.

"So she can't have no variety? She supposed to drink that same powdered shit day after day?"

37

"Babies drink formula or breast milk. That's it," Leesa said, and turned to Malikia, frowning. "I can't tell you how much money she could save me if she'd just take it from the tap."

"Don't nobody want to hear about your booby-milk sob story, Leesa," Hakiam said.

Leesa grabbed the box that he was eating from. "You didn't leave me one freaking french fry! And I'll talk about my boobies if I want to." She gave him a nudge on the side of his head. "Now what am I going to do for dinner?"

"Get your hand out of my face, Leesa. I'm sure that place you got that burger from is still open."

"Oh, so it's up to me to buy some more food."

"Yeah, you. If the check from social services don't come on time, you got to have another plan. You can't just stand around here starving. You better—"

"Hold up," she told him. "I know you ain't trying to holler to me about all what I should do in my apartment."

"You mean the HUDs, don't you?"

She walked the empty box over to the trash can. "You got all the mouth in the world. It ain't your place to say nothing about nothing."

He waved her away. "It ain't too much to ask that you have something here to eat."

"You want something so bad, then why don't you walk your happy ass down to the store and get it and quit giving me a shitload of drama about it? Shit, Hakiam, you're supposed to be helping me out."

"I am, ain't I?"

38

"Big help you are sitting around here eating what you know was my food."

"You promised me that I could have room and board."

"I said room."

"You said board, too."

"I know what I said, Hakiam."

"Well, I ain't even got room. I got couch. You got the only room."

"Listen, I don't got to put up with this from you. My mom offered to take Malikia in—"

"Well, maybe you ought to let her do it."

"Maybe you ought to shut your mouth and be grateful you got a roof over your head."

About this time Malikia started wailing. Leesa checked her T-shirt to see a big wet stain on it.

"Goddamnit," she said. "She got me again. That's the second time today."

All Hakiam wanted was a life with no sharp hard places. He wished he could get his own apartment. Someplace by himself. A two-bedroom: one to sleep in and one for entertainment. You know, shoot pool, lift weights, just chill. Then he thought, *Why stop there?* If he was going to dream, he was going to dream big. How about having a big mansion all to himself, with aluminum siding and big picture windows with pressed drapes and a long driveway surrounded by bushes trimmed into perfect rectangles? That was a much better vision than fiddling around some dinky, falling-apart hood apartment waiting on some government cheese.

He left Cincinnati for this? He could have saved himself the seventy-five-dollar bus fare and the bumpy ride he'd never forget.

Only a couple of weeks into this arrangement and it already stank like rotting flesh. It was like being in a marriage. A bad one where all he argued about was money (and the lack thereof). They would go round and round about the emptines of the icebox, and cable TV (she claimed she "needed" it; he thought it was a waste and would rather have Internet access), and the electricchargecardbill, and the heattelephonebill, and on and on. And where did she get off nudging the side of his head? No, it didn't hurt, but it was the way she did it. No respect. Not a damn bit of respect. Let him put his hands on her just once and he bet she'd turn it into a federal case. The paltriness of his life ran through his mind, keeping him from sleep.

After another hour, he started hearing a driving beat and laughter and loud talk. He got up and walked into the front room. He nodded. No wonder Leesa had said it was okay for him to sleep in her room. There was a noisy, crowded party that seemed like it had first been confined to the kitchenette but had now spilled out into the hallway.

He made his way over to his cousin, who was in the kitchen, and asked her how come she hadn't told him about this.

"I hope you ain't think I got to run everything by you. This is my place, remember—my place," she yelled, almost losing her balance.

40

Hakiam rolled his eyes. Leesa was so drunk, she was practically in a state of collapse.

"Hey, how's Philly treating you?" some guy asked.

Someone else offered him a taste. Hakiam had nothing against alcohol, so he took a swallow or two.

Hakiam thought he better stay up just to keep an eye on Leesa. Especially since the party was at a weird stage, the part when the club atmosphere expanded to a bursting point and more and more people started coming in. The music kept on going. That beat had a life of its own. Plenty of faces, but each face felt like one he'd seen many times. How could that be? He'd only been there for a few weeks.

And then he saw her. *Her.* She looked like she'd just walked off the cover of one of those booty books. She had a pair of ripe butt cheeks that stared at him from her red hot pants, and when she turned back around he saw more of her anatomy. Nice tight waist, gorgeous high-shelved breasts. Big smile. A little too toothy and spacey, but hey, when you have a body like that who needs a good face?

Was it he who glided over to her or vice versa? It all happened so fast. He found out her name was Yasmine and that she lived just a few blocks away, on Fifty-first and Claire Street.

Hakiam was all ready to throw in. He was about to get into deep conversation with this fine thing. Since he'd been in this City of Brotherly Love, he hadn't gone out with one honey. He was well overdue for some affection. Could she be the one? Could that emptiness all end right here and now?

41

He reached out to pull a strand of her weave from her eyes, and she kind of tossed her head back and did a laugh as he told her his name and that he liked her outfit, what little there was of it.

But then, out of the corner of his eye he saw this dude roll up on them. He was cut, like he spent a lot of time in a gym (the kind that required a membership or the kind that they have in the penitentiary). He had a certain masculine candor of "if you keep messing with my girl you're going to find yourself getting up off the floor."

Hakiam hated when guys got like that, all stingy. He'd seen this a thousand times. She presents herself as a free agent, but in reality, she's locked into a contract that can't be broken.

That dude gave him a second heavy look, and Hakiam wasn't going to wait for a third.

That was when he decided to call it a night. It had to be a record for the shortest time he'd ever spent at a party.

He went into the back room and collapsed on his cousin's bed next to Malikia. She was no fool; this baby had her little hands drawn up to her ears now to shield them from the sounds.

That made him chuckle a bit, that the infant wasn't a fan of hip-hop—maybe she'd be into jazz. One thing was for sure, at least: she could sleep. Hakiam went back to spending his would-be rest doing the proverbial tossing and turning as night melted back into day.

10

Was there anything worse than being seen out in public with your parent? And at a mall, no less. A mall that was heavily trafficked by kids from your school. Wendy's father was there with Wendy in tow to buy winter curtains for the front room, which meant that they were deep in the department-store wing. At least none of her peers hung out there. Still, Wendy had to endure her father's analysis paralysis as he looked at each swatch and fragment, comparing not size, not color, not texture, but cost.

Wendy eyed a pin-striped set and pointed it out to her father. "Eighty-one dollars. Forget it!" he exclaimed.

The woman at the counter wore a strained smile. She blew air into her bangs as she looked over at him. Wendy wondered if the woman had any other customers that threw such a conniption so easily.

He asked the saleswoman, "Why is this pattern four dollars more?"

The woman tried to explain. Wendy and her father had been there for the past forty minutes; people had bought new cars in less time.

They say you should let your emotions out little by little, so that you don't explode all of a sudden. Wendy attempted to keep that in mind as her father asked, "Couldn't you knock off twenty percent?"

"I'm sorry, sir, the price is as marked," the woman said.

"How about fifteen?"

"I can't do that, sir."

Wendy bit off a hangnail as her dad, ever the persistent one, continued, "How about ten? A ten percent discount. You offer that when people open a line of credit here, don't you?"

"Do you want to open a line of credit?" the woman asked.

"No, I would just like to have the ten percent."

"For God's sake, Dad," Wendy said. "How many different ways are you going to ask for the same thing? She can't give you a discount; the price is as marked. Why are you so cheap?"

"Because he's a man," the saleswoman answered.

After they left the store, her father commented, "That was very unprofessional, making a statement like that."

"Let it go, Dad."

"I'm never going back in that store again."

"Sure, Dad."

"There are two other department stores in this mall."

"So you plan to haggle them to death instead?"

"Young lady, I do not have to put up with rude service and high prices. That store must think I've never seen a curtain before."

"I wish I hadn't," Wendy said. She noticed a few people her age passing by on the other side of the aisle. Upon a closer look, she realized they weren't her classmates and breathed a sigh of relief.

She and her father ended up in the rotunda.

There was a sign posted that said JONATHAN DANIELS SINGS EVERY THURSDAY. It sounded like a threat. But sure enough, an acoustic guitarist was set up there, singing his own cryptic lyrics with a small crowd gathered around him. He sang in a pseudo-sincere, sandy voice. There was also a table full of CDs for passersby to purchase if they liked what they heard.

Around the center court, there was a gathering mainly made up of slightly bemused senior citizens with their arms folded in judgment. Way, way up front stood an enraptured female fan with hungry eyes. Her hands were laced together in prayer. Now, why was she so supportive? Wendy wondered. Was she a girlfriend? Manager? Sister? Creditor?

"Come on, Dad, let's go," Wendy said.

Her dad, however, was in a groove. "Now, that's what I call singing. Not a lot of shouting and gyrating. No filthy lyrics like those ignorant rappers that get played on the radio."

"Let's go, Dad."

But Mr. Anderson wasn't budging. He seemed to really like this James Blunt rip-off.

"I'll be in the food court," Wendy told her father, and went on her way.

She got a slice of gourmet pizza and a soda and found an out-of-the-way table with an umbrella over it for further cover.

When her father came along he asked, "What did they put on your slice?"

"Zucchini."

He frowned. "That's brilliant."

She frowned too. "Want some, Dad?"

He shook his head and told her he was in the mood for a California roll. Wendy watched him go over to the Sushi-to-Go line.

Wendy took another bite of her pizza. At the table beside her, there was a group of sales associates from Radio Shack. They were talking about mobile phones.

At another nearby table, a couple was making moon eyes at each other over a hot fudge sundae.

"Oh, hi, Wendy," someone said. She turned her head to see not just one person she knew, but three: Rhea, Jillian, and Carlyle.

Wendy suppressed her gag reflex. Of all the girls she had to run into, why did it have to be them, the three most psycho people she knew?

Wendy didn't bother to say hello. She just turned her head back in the other direction.

"Nice to see you out," Rhea said.

It was clear to Wendy that they wouldn't go off on their own. They would keep lingering and bothering her.

"Who are you here with?" Jillian asked.

"Yeah, I didn't know you were dating anyone," Carlyle said in that childlike bobbing way she had of talking.

"Who's the lucky guy?" Rhea asked.

"Get out of my face, you three bitches," Wendy told them. But before that sting had a chance to sink in, her dad had come back with his platter. "Hello, young ladies."

They were so cute with their phony-baloney smiles, their hair drawn up in high ponytails, and their jiggling charm bracelets (which, at sixteen and seventeen, they still hadn't outgrown). It was no surprise that any parent would think they were sweetness incarnate. It seemed like forever before they slipped away in their ballet flats.

"They seem like such nice girls," her father said. "Why don't you ever invite them over?"

Wendy didn't answer. It wasn't just the haughty countenance they had or the silly, tiny, swingy skirts they always wore that irked her. In Wendy's opinion, they were evil. Pure evil, plain and simple. They weren't like the other in-crowd girls, who let her off easy by ignoring her. No, they got their kicks from downing other people. It was Rhea and company who started the rumor years ago that Wendy's mother had OD'd. Thanks to them, half the school thought her mom had been on street drugs; the other half believed she'd committed suicide. Wendy's mother had actually passed away as a result of a bad reaction to prescription drugs. She had been only thirty six years old, but did that matter to Rhea and company? It was all fair game to giggle and whisper behind someone's back.

Wendy could only dread what they would concoct at school tomorrow. Probably some story about how they saw Wendy with her father in some weird incestuous embrace. They always had to spice up their gossip, make everything gross and sexy—plain facts would never do.

Her father was still singing their praises, suggesting that they come over that weekend. It wasn't too cold out to heat up the gas grill.

Take slow, deep breaths, Wendy. Take slow, deep breaths, she told herself.

"I could make some kabobs," he said.

Wendy thought for a moment, *Why not tell him what they did?* But that notion was fleeting. She didn't tell him about things like that. She didn't talk to her father about anything, really; they just argued about curtains, zucchini, and the ghetto.

She swirled her crushed ice around with her straw till her father told her to quit.

After a while, they got up, stacked their trays, and made their way toward the exit. They passed a store called the Child's Boutique. At that moment, Hakiam popped into her mind—and that weird, convoluted tale he had told her.

"I want to stop in here," she told her dad.

"What in heaven's name for?"

Wendy ignored the question and walked into the primary-colors-dominated store. Everything was so bright and shiny. As her father trailed behind her, he asked who was pregnant.

"No one's pregnant, Dad. She already had the baby."

"Who? Who? Who had a baby?"

"Nobody you know."

But her father kept stalking her. By the crib mobile section of the store, she finally told him that she was looking for something nice for this little girl from the tutoring center.

"I wasn't aware that you were tutoring people that young, Wendy."

"I'm not, Dad. Look, I don't want to go into it. It's confusing. There's a baby that I want to welcome into the world, end of story."

He shook his head in disgust. "She's probably one of nine. You know how much *those women* like to have babies."

"What difference does it make if she has a lot of siblings? She still deserves a welcome, Dad."

They'd reached the clothing section. She found a really pretty one-piece outfit with little strawberries and ruffles on it.

Her father hovered. "You know, it's a colossal waste of time, effort, and money to get anything nice for people like that."

With that comment, it was decided.

"I'll take it," Wendy said. She walked to the register and slid her credit card over the counter.

11

Something about sleeping right through his second day of class reminded Hakiam of old times. Those lazy, hazy days of his previous school years, where he coasted the waves of trig, lit, and Western civ without ever getting wet. He was glad this center wasn't the kind of place where the teachers came circling about asking loaded questions like "Are you feeling all right?" if they found a head down on a desk. So that was how the first half of his day went, smooth as butter. Not a soul hassled him.

At the end of his "classes," he felt refreshed and bright-eyed. Then it was time to meet up with *her* again.

He was all set to bust her chops some more, but as he approached the tutoring center, he didn't find that cute brown-skinned, overdressed, prissy thing sitting in her usual spot. He didn't see her anywhere.

"Where's that girl?" he asked a sandy-haired guy sitting at a table.

"She called in sick today."

Hakiam figured the man was about his age, and got the sinking feeling that he was not just a substitute but a replacement.

"Will she be back tomorrow?"

"I don't know. What subject do you need help with?" the young man asked, then offered a wide smile and said, "Maybe I can help."

Hakiam didn't bother to answer. Instead, he sought the nearest exit.

Throughout his short life, one of Hakiam's main hobbies had always been roaming the streets. He could walk for hours. That afternoon, since he had nothing else to do, he wound up around what the yuppies called University City because this was the area where the Penn and Drexel students were housed. It was a breezy fall day. On the outskirts of the campuses there were Asian groceries, a flower stand run by a one-legged woman, a few peanut stands, and a pretzel stand. The vendor running the latter had a string of pretzels shoved into his armpit. He broke them off one by one as people ordered them. Hakiam figured the armpit just added to the salty flavor.

Hakiam passed the brownstones with ivy hugging every brick, and he wondered whether one day those plants could bring a building down.

He walked a few more blocks, cutting through Penn's campus. It soured him to view this parade of purposeful people of various heights, sizes, and nationalities, all walking with such vigor. To Hakiam, they were show-offs, carrying their thick books. They reminded him of how he had grown weary of doing nothing day after day. He wished again that that annoying girl had been there at the tutoring center. Messing with her was a fun diversion.

There was a clothing store just beyond the walkway that sold sweats and jeans. As soon as Hakiam entered, bells seemed to go off. It was like they could smell his brokeness. Wasn't that why they followed him around? He wondered fleetingly if the result would have been any different if he had shoes with shoestrings or his pants weren't saggy or his hoodie wasn't up. This was practically the shoplifter's uniform.

The security guard had a heavy profile but a light walk. He was good at his job and tried to make it look casual. He whistled a pleasant tune that Hakiam didn't recognize and trailed him like a shadow.

Finally, while Hakiam was weaving past the jacket rack, the guard asked the very loaded question: "Can I help you?"

Hakiam up-and-downed the brother before answering. "Yeah," he said, holding up a blazer, "you can pay for this for me."

Back on the street, he started thinking that black men had basically cornered the market on the security-guard industry. It made perfect sense, in a way. A black person was far less likely to be accused of hassling other blacks than someone of another race was. It was hard to imagine a discrimination case going anywhere. So this kind of hovering went on, and there was really no redress.

In all fairness, Hakiam had been known to steal,

especially when he was low on paper, like he was now. But he would never be stupid enough to do it in a place that had sensory detectors and exploding dye. Since he'd moved to Philly, this was the first time his other longtime hobby—purse snatching—had crossed his mind.

He tried to think of something else as he crossed the footbridge into downtown. He thought of what dinner would be like if he had funds. He daydreamed of a beautiful spread: buttered rolls, collards, potato salad, candied yams, spinach, and generous portions of moist, flavorful meat loaf.

Just then a small-framed woman passed by him. She looked about thirty and wore high-heeled pumps. She was wrapped up in her cell phone conversation, not paying attention at all to her large purple handbag, which was loose on her shoulder. Odds were she had about fifty bucks in there, at least. Maybe an iPod or a BlackBerry. She probably carried some gift cards on her, and, of course, credit cards.

If only it weren't so easy, Hakiam thought as he moved closer to her. All it would take was one grab and a quick jog in the other direction. Even if she chased him, she could barely keep up for more than two blocks, and that was if she wanted to take her shoes off.

Hakiam was just about to reach for it. He got closer and closer, thinking, *So much for a fresh start in a new city.* And what difference did it make, anyway? This lady could probably afford it. It would be just a little skin off her back, but to him, it was a few square meals, maybe a movie at the cineplex, and some freedom.

He told himself, *Take it. Just take it. Grab it now and run.* But then she turned to him, clutching her bag extra tight, and a mean look formed on her otherwise pretty face. *How could she know?*

He tried to look innocent.

She kept her visage stony and made sure he moved ahead of her.

Shit, he thought. Now he was really down. He felt like he was hanging by a burning rope. He wondered if everyone in Philly could read his mind. That was supposed to be simple: Bag Swiping 101. If he couldn't fall back on his old tricks, what did he have left?

12

"I missed you the other day," he said.

"Are you speaking to me?"

Hakiam casually jerked his chin toward the seat next to her and said, "No, I'm talking to the chair."

Wendy's cheeks grew warm and she thought of giving him a straight answer. Instead, she opted for a wisecrack. "I'd be interested to know when the chair responds."

He scooted into the spot next to her.

She still didn't meet his eye.

He pulled out a book entitled *American History After 1865*. Her Hershey bar–colored eyes met his. "Do you want to work or kid around, Hakiam?"

"Work, I guess," he mumbled.

Wendy rolled her shoulders back. She opened up his book. "You haven't cracked this, have you?"

"How can you tell, cuz the pages look new?"

"No, because the book made a cracking sound."

He reached in his pocket and pulled out a piece of paper. He ironed the creases out of it and handed it to her.

"Oh, this is your syllabus. It says you're supposed to read pages 233 to 267. Have you read 233 to 267?"

"Nope."

"Well then, why don't you come back when you've read 233 to 267."

He shrugged. She watched him place the syllabus in the book then close it, knowing that that was the most exercise it had had since it had been in his possession.

"Do you want to be a teacher? Is that why you volunteer here?" he asked her.

"No, I'm going to be a doctor."

"Why would a good-looking girl like you want to be cooped up in some hospital all day?"

Was that some kind of mixed-up compliment? she wondered as she answered his question with a question. "Everyone who works in a hospital is good-looking; don't you watch *Grey's Anatomy*?"

Instead of laughing, he smirked at that. "Bet you have to go to school for a long time to be a doctor."

"Yes, that's correct."

"How long?"

"Four years after you graduate college, then four years of residency, so all together I'll be tied up for twelve."

"Damn. You want to spend all that time in school?"

"Yes," she said. "Unlike you, I like opening books."

He smirked again, only this time it was a looser expression, less self-conscious.

He took his book and rose from his seat. He was almost to the stairs when she stopped him. "Oh, I almost forgot," she said, and pulled out a bright pink gift bag.

"What's that?" he asked.

"I thought this would be nice for that girl that hangs around you getting a contact high. Here." She held out the bag.

He walked up to her and looked in. He pulled out the onesie with the strawberries and the ruffles and put it up to his chest. "It doesn't fit," he said.

She grinned. He averted his eyes.

He took the present and the next thing she heard was his footsteps as he walked down the stairs.

There was a PC in the corner. She went over to it and checked her e-mails. There was nothing all that important. Two were from Erin. Some e-coupons and newsletters. She heard footsteps again, so she shut down the computer and went back to her table.

Two tutees in one session? That's a record, she thought.

But as it turned out, she had rearranged herself for nothing. It was only Hakiam. "What do you want?" she asked him.

He gestured to the bag and said, "You're all right."

She chuckled a little. "You're welcome." She always thought it was funny when people had trouble saying simple words like "please" or "thank you."

She expected him to depart again, but instead he just

stood there with his eyes drilling into her. Suddenly, her creep-alert flag went up. *Why isn't he leaving? Why are he and his ill-fitting clothes still hanging around?*

"Is there something else you want to say?" she asked.

He opened his mouth, then closed it. Then opened it again and said, "You want to go out for a cup of coffee?"

"You mean *coffee* coffee?"

"Yeah."

"You and me?" she asked.

"Yeah," he said.

"You are sure you mean *us*?"

He nodded.

"Well," she began, "my time's just about up here."

She wrapped a scarf about her neck, grabbed her canvas bag, and stood up.

Then they descended the steep stairs and left the building.

13

He had a five on him. He scanned the menu list above the register. There was eggnog latte, peppermint patty hot chocolate, chocolate-covered-cherry cappuccino, and pecan pie coffee. He kept looking and looking for the plain stuff in the hopes that it would be cheaper. Plus, these specialties all came in foreign-language sizes. How little was a venti? How big was a grande? Why couldn't they just say small, medium, and large?

"I'll have a tall half caf, leave room for cream, please," Wendy said.

The barista, who had an exaggerated flip to her hair and an easy smile, nodded, then looked at Hakiam for his order.

He thought fast and said, "Nothing."

The barista's sunny smile didn't lapse. She went to make Wendy's order.

"Don't you want a water, at least?" Wendy asked Hakiam.

He shook his head without meeting her eyes.

There was a couple of dollars and change in the tip cup—talk about courting robbery. That was something you'd never see down the other end of Lancaster Avenue. Everything that could be stolen was kept under lock and key.

The girl with the flip to her hair came back with Wendy's drink. They headed for seats.

Wendy wasn't a tall girl, but she had a long, slender back, which Hakiam enjoyed watching as he walked behind her. Since there were no more tables available, they took seats on the sofa by the window.

Wendy set her cup on the end table. "Funny, when you asked me for coffee, I was sure you were going to have some too."

Hakiam gave a half grin and put a dollar and change back in his pocket.

Wendy took a sip and asked him, "Don't you like coffee?"

"I've never done this before," he said.

"You've never done what before?"

He looked at her hard for a good moment or two, then said, "Skip it."

She observed him for an equally long period of time and said, "I'm not sure what I'm supposed to be skipping."

Silence.

More silence.

Wendy stirred her coffee.

More silence.

Hakiam looked outside. The coffee shop was on the corner of a busy intersection. The light had just changed and a mass of people trekked from one side of the street to the other. He peered back at Wendy with a blank, washed-out expression. This was an improvement, because he was doing his best to suppress the scowl that he customarily wore.

"So," she said, "what's your favorite movie?"

"Huh?"

"What's—your—favorite—movie?" she said again, slowing down her words.

He still had no answer.

"Mine is *Twelve Angry Men*," she said.

There was another pause. Then, she started carrying on a conversation with herself that went like this:

"What's that about, Wendy?

"Well, I'm glad you asked me that, Hakiam. *Twelve Angry Men* is about a jury that believes it has an open-and-shut case. But one juror—Henry Fonda, he plays the architect—he thinks that the young person on trial for murder deserves at least some deliberation and votes not guilty.

"Why is that your favorite movie, Wendy?

"Well, I'm glad you asked, Hakiam. It comes on American Movie Classics all the time. I like issue-oriented films, like that one and *The Ox-Bow Incident* and *Inherit the Wind*."

At that point, she ran out of steam. She seemed weary of all the back-and-forth with herself.

He gave her another blank look.

61

She frowned. "You probably go for fast cars over character development."

"No, I'm listening," he assured her.

"I also liked *Boyz n the Hood.*"

"What are you doing watching that?"

"I told you, I like issue-oriented movies."

"What was the issue in that?"

"Senseless street violence, poverty, the high homicide rate among young African American men . . ."

"You need a movie to tell you that? You ain't know nobody who was murdered?"

"No. You do?"

"I know a couple."

Wendy wanted to ask the who, what, where, and why. Instead, she just took another sip of her coffee.

Hakiam stared at the way Wendy's beige-colored lipstick left a half kiss on the rim of her cup and sighed.

More silence. "You go to church?" he asked.

"Not since my mother died. Why do you ask?"

"I don't know. I was just asking things like you were asking things."

"Do you go to church, Hakiam?"

"Hell, no."

Wendy laughed until she realized she was laughing all alone and then said, "That was a joke, right?"

More silence, then he said, "Yeah."

"When I did go, I went with my mom. She was Catholic, but my dad was raised Baptist."

"Oh. Might have guessed that you came from a mixed marriage."

She chuckled this time, not caring that she was alone. She waited a beat or two more before saying, "You ought to do stand-up."

More silence. He glanced out the window again.

She looked at the clock. It was almost five.

She snapped her fingers as a thought occurred to her. "You know, that just might be the answer."

"What?" he asked.

"Church. They would love someone like you."

"What do you mean by that?"

"I mean there are people in this world who live to help out. When I was looking for a place to volunteer, I ran into a lot of places with a religious link."

"My aunt is one of those people. She's always saying things like 'God is good.'"

"God is good," Wendy repeated.

"'All the time,' she says."

"Well," Wendy said sarcastically. "Nobody's perfect. Why don't you stay with her instead of your present arrangement?"

"I don't know. She's really changed now that she found religion. Do you know how many rules them Bible people have? That's why my cousin can't live with her. I don't want a bunch of rules."

"I don't see how it could be any worse."

"I don't see how it's no better."

Wendy rolled her eyes. "What are you talking about? A curfew?"

He laughed. "That's just the start."

"How do you know?"

"Because I do," he told her.

"What's your aunt's name?"

"Josephine."

"Aunt Josephine, eh?" Wendy mused aloud. "You don't want to run the streets here. Philadelphia has some of the highest crime rates in the country. You don't need the fast lane. Where does your aunt live?"

"She's on Catharine Street."

"That's not far."

"I know."

"You should live with her instead of your cousin. She sounds much more stable."

Hakiam shook his head. "It's not for me. I ain't looking for a mother. I'll be eighteen soon."

Wendy's eyes held him in a steady gaze. "Hakiam, take it from me. Everyone needs a mother. Everyone in the whole world."

Her cell rang. She put it to her ear and said, without even checking it, "Yes, Dad. . . . I'm in a coffee shop. . . . I'm drinking coffee. . . . Never mind that."

She rolled her eyes.

"Okay. . . . I won't forget. . . . You said Visine. . . . Write it down?"

She stepped up her voice.

"I don't have to write it down! I'll remember to pick it up. . . . I'll be home soon. . . . When do you think *soon* is? . . . In an hour. . . . I will pick up your Murine—I mean, Visine. Goodbye."

She slipped the phone back into her tote bag.

"I better go." She held up the cup and said a half sentence before leaving: "Thanks for the . . ."

And then she was gone.

Gone. It seemed like they had just come in. Hakiam had hardly had the chance to say or do what he really wanted. He was going to brush his knee against hers—if he'd had a few more moments. He was going to lean close and whisper in her ear, perhaps. He was going to do *something*. He was. If only he had had a little more time.

14

When Wendy told Erin she had gone out with some-one from the tutoring center that afternoon, Erin summed up things with: "How Bill Clinton of you!"

"What do you mean by that?" Wendy asked.

"Well, he got it on with his intern," Erin said.

"Erin, *I'm* the intern."

"Okay then, how Monica Lewinsky."

A mental picture popped into Wendy's mind and she said, "Oh, God. That's not what's happening. This was a G-rated get-together."

"Well, even if it wasn't. It's not like you're a teacher. If you were a teacher and he were your student and you two had feelings for each other, now, that would be icky."

"Who said anything about feelings? We just went for coffee, and he didn't even have that."

"What did he order?"

"Nothing. He just sat there. He barely said a word, Erin."

"Oh, so he's the strong, silent type."

"That's one way to look at it."

"He was probably nervous, you know, first date and all."

"First date?"

"Yes, first of many, Wendy. Didn't I tell you this would happen? I mean, you kept talking and talking and *talking* about him."

"Nothing happened, Erin."

"Will you quit it already?"

"Okay, I guess I like the way he challenges. We spar and joust with each other. I guess sooner or later that's bound to get to you."

"Yeah, either you fall in love or kill each other."

"This isn't love. I just like his kind of humor."

"He's dry?"

"Yeah, he's real dry."

"So he's funny. I love funny guys. Especially when they're cute, but that almost never happens— Hold on, Wendy, my call-waiting just beeped."

Erin clicked over to the other line, and Wendy paced the kitchen, which ridiculously well-ordered. No Cheerios strewn on the counter, no dirty plates or saucers brimming from the sink. There was a place for everything, and, thanks to her father, everything knew its place. Even the top of the fridge was dust-free. She walked to the other end of the kitchen and glanced in the trash, and it was there that she saw a large envelope addressed to her, unopened. She retrieved it and her eye shot to the upper left-hand corner: *Howard University*.

Wendy felt her face heat up.

Erin came back on the line, saying, "We ought to double-date. Me, you, Hakiam, and Kyle."

Wendy couldn't focus on something so innocent as double-dating. Her father had done it again! Once again, he'd violated her trust.

"Erin, I'll have to call you back," she said, and flipped her cell closed.

Wendy went straight upstairs to her father's room only to find it empty. The TV was on, though, playing an ad for a luxury car pitched by a thirtysomething woman in a tight satin dress.

Wendy left the bedroom and spotted her dad in the bathroom, standing in front of the sink. He dabbed his face with a washcloth, then dotted both his eyes with Visine.

He blinked.

She scowled.

He turned to her. "I want to thank you for picking up the right brand, Wendy."

Now she was really boiling. He was too much! To the world he looked like a standard-issue "harmless" dad— fortyish, bespectacled, and balding, doing what most widowed dads would do at eight at night: watching TV and grooming himself during commercials. But Wendy knew he was anything but ordinary and innocent. He went through her library books, once calling a text by W.E.B. Du Bois "militant and revolutionary." He had returned *The Souls of Black Folk* for her long before it was due. Wendy remembered thinking that there should be a law against things like that. Ironically, she knew the Patriot Act had introduced a rule to the opposite effect: librarians were supposed to report "questionable" books that the public took out. Say, if someone had a stack of how-to-build-a-bomb books, librarians were supposed to comply and submit that patron's name to the authorities. Luckily, Patriot Act be damned, some librarians would rather go to jail than betray their patrons' right to read whatever book they wanted.

Yet her dad was at it again, the self-appointed secretary of Homeland Security. Now he'd taken to seizing her mail.

"You threw out my letter," she said.

He offered his daughter a very monotone "Yes." Then he excused himself and went back to his room.

Her dad lived for American Movie Classics. A James Cagney movie was on. Wendy didn't absorb enough of his performance to tell if Cagney was on the wrong or right side of the law. She knew enough about the actor to know that he wore a trench coat regardless of whether he was a crook or a cop.

Her dad took his seat five feet from the TV screen.

She hated when he played her off cool like that.

"You have no right to throw my things away!" she shouted at him. "I want to go to a historically black college."

"Over my dead body," he replied.

"Dad, my going to an HBC is not going to kill you."

"And you're sure of that?" He reached for his cup and stirred his evening tea, then took a sip.

"There's nothing wrong with going to a black college. Plenty of successful people have done it."

He laughed and said, "Name three."

"Easily," she said. "The astronaut Ronald McNair. The *60 Minutes* commentator Ed Bradley. And, last but not least, Oprah Winfrey."

"All flukes."

"Dad, come on."

"This is my house, Wendy. I have a right to discard anything I don't want in it."

"Why are you such a control freak?"

"I just told you this is my house."

"I'm sixteen years old."

"You are my daughter before anything else; I don't care if you're sixty. And one thing's for sure, Barack Obama didn't go to a black college."

"No, Dad, he just went to Reverend Jeremiah Wright's church."

"He was never present for those radical speeches!"

"Denial is more than a river in Africa, Dad."

"Wendy, Barack Obama is clean and articulate."

"Where have I heard that before?"

"No one could confuse President Obama with some gangster. You are not going to a black school. I do not want you around that element."

"What element—college students?"

"They are not college students."

She shook the brochure in his face. "I guess it's a mirage, then."

"You're going backward, Wendy. This isn't the nineteen-twenties. Those schools were created because we weren't allowed to go to the regular schools. They were a consolation prize. They are secondary. You can now go to the regular schools, and that, Wendy, is what I plan for you to do."

"Why can't I go to the school I want to go to?"

"How do you expect me to rest nights with my mind racing with thoughts of you, my only child, in the atmosphere of drive-bys, dope addicts, and hos?"

"Hos?" she asked. "What makes you so sure there are hos at Howard?"

"I MapQuested that school, Wendy. It's right by the projects."

"It's also near the Capitol. Did MapQuest tell you that, too, Dad?"

"Young lady, a lot of people don't have any choices, but you do. I've sent you to the finest schools. You're groomed for the Ivy League."

"Translation: I have been cooped up with white people for the past eleven years."

"Be that as it may, a lot of people would kill to attend the schools you've gone to. You should be grateful—"

"I am grateful. I value my education, Dad."

"Then it's settled. You will not go to Howard or any other black college. I'm not going to let you do this. I want you to be around safe, predictable people. You are

71

not going to worry me into an early grave risking your life around those people."

"Why do you keep saying 'those people'?"

"You're not a child, Wendy. I don't have to explain everything to you."

"You're not explaining anything to me. You're talking like a lunatic."

His voice rose. "How dare you call your father a lunatic!"

"I said you were talking like a lunatic, I didn't say you were one, Dad."

"I have a right to my beliefs."

"They are not very informed beliefs. Anyone can tell you that Howard is a selective school."

"Don't make me laugh."

"It *is,* Dad."

"Look, there was a time when the black community carried itself with dignity and class. We turned out Nat King Cole and Harry Belafonte. Now what do we have? Snoop Dogg and Ice Cube."

"What does that have to do with me going to the college I want?"

"I have sent you to the finest private schools. You could have your pick. You could go to one of the Seven Sister schools!"

"So it's all right for me to go to a women's college but not a black college?"

"Exactly."

"Why?"

"Think of your future. What would an employer think? Don't stigmatize yourself unnecessarily."

"Any place of employment that would think like that is a place I wouldn't be comfortable working for anyway!"

"This is getting very circular. Wendy, I am not going to argue all night. You don't need to apply to one of those schools. Choose another. There are thousands of others. You may think this is what you want, but you are just going through a phase."

"This is not a phase!" Wendy pointed to her father's skin.

He shook his head. "The future, Wendy, is not black."

15

When Hakiam got to the apartment, he found Malikia in a car seat. This struck Hakiam as strange because Leesa didn't have a car. But there the baby was, propped in the seat by the plastic-covered couch. The TV was blaring a video that was heavy with the b word, and the air was heavy with the smell of fried hair. Leesa brushed past him with a new hairdo, which was shoulder-length and all of a sudden straight and swishy. He also noticed she had a new tattoo. It was the word "mother" stenciled into the center of her back.

"Where did you get that?" he asked his cousin, pointing to the car seat.

"They were giving them away at the social services center."

Hakiam walked over to the seat and rocked it with his foot. At first, Malikia seemed amused, but within seconds, she got fussy and broke into her customary low cry.

"Why didn't you leave well enough alone?" Leesa asked him.

Malikia started crying harder, and Hakiam thought, *Babies are such wimps*. They needed an endless supply of petting and hugs. Constant soothing.

"This world is rough," he told Malikia. "So you gotta be tough."

"Great advice," Leesa said before going back into the bathroom. "How do you like my hair?"

"It's unbeweavable, Goldilocks. Don't you have to work tonight?"

"Nope."

The voice from the TV changed to another rapper. The radiator coughed. The streetlight sliced through the blinds, making horizontal lines across the room.

Some kids down the hall were playing with a ball and paddle. It made a repetitive sound. *Thump. Thump. Thump.*

Next door, a plate broke when it hit the floor. "Shit," someone said.

Hakiam heard another bang from the hall and went out to investigate.

He saw two kids, about four or five years old, who had set down the ball and paddle and were playing in the trash chute, sticking their heads in. Hakiam considered running over and telling them to stop, but he soon nixed the idea. They looked like the type that would kick Hakiam in the shins rather than listen.

He went back inside and took an extra blanket from Leesa's room. He grabbed a pillow and arranged it on the armchair. He took a look over at Malikia in her car seat on the floor. She started crying.

"Darn you," Hakiam told her.

That really got her open, toothless mouth to bawling. *Here we go again.*

Leesa walked by him, smelling of a Giorgio perfume knockoff.

"You going out?" he asked her.

"Yep."

"Who you going out with?"

"What's it to you?" she snapped.

He plunked his feet on the end table, closed his eyes, and nearly fell asleep. Then he jumped up and said, "I almost forgot." He retrieved the bag that Wendy had given him.

Leesa stopped in her tracks. "Where did you get that from?" she asked.

"The girl."

"What girl?"

"The girl from the center."

Leesa's eyes went back to the gift. She curled her lip at him and said, "What makes her think I want her charity?"

"You want everybody else's," he muttered.

Leesa took the outfit out of the bag. She held the onesie to her as a half smile leaked out. She looked at her daughter, then back at her cousin.

"So, you like this girl?"

He shrugged. "She's all right."

"She got an extra room?"

16

L ife is an issue of circumstance.

All Wendy knew of life was living in a primarily white area, attending primarily white schools, and associating with primarily white people.

Like the only chip in the cookie, she was used to it, but that didn't mean she felt comfortable. And though she had never been asked explicitly "What's it like being the only black girl in class?" she had an answer ready in her head.

So what's it really like?

It's like not getting invited to a birthday party.

It's like not being invited to a birthday party for a person you know just as well as the people who are invited.

It's like not being invited to a birthday party for a person you know just as well as the people who are invited right in front of you, as if you were invisible.

Invisible, not in the way little kids fantasized about, but like Ralph Ellison described in his famous book.

Most people thought that being a different color would make everyone see you. Actually, it was just the opposite. You were more likely to be ignored. You got talked about like you were just not there.

When Wendy was young, it affected her more, but as she'd gotten older she could choose her company a little better. She befriended Erin and Erin befriended her, and somehow when you had one person at school who you could really trust and relate to, life was livable.

But that didn't mean that there weren't still times.

After spring break last term, Wendy had walked past a group of girls who were discussing their vacation to Cancún. They had their forearms side by side, and were comparing their tans and telling each other:

"You are black."

"No, you are black."

"No, no, you *are black."*

Wendy remembered thinking, *If only it were that simple.* Color was the easy part. Black was also a culture. Wendy doubted that these girls ever had black-eyed peas to welcome in the New Year or danced the pop and lock at a family picnic. And beyond cultural expressions, she wondered if these girls had any concept of consciousness. Did they know anything about Angela Davis or Sally Hemmings? Or were they stuck in a one-dimensional experience of race? A pigeonholing, based on sight only.

The hope of gaining a more complete understanding of her race had led Wendy to volunteer at the center. Today marked her two-month anniversary.

When Wendy saw Hakiam approach, she slipped a

bookmark into her schoolbook and set it before her on the table. She wore a lace-inset tank top, low-rise jeans, and a crocheted wrap as a belt.

"You look different," Hakiam told her.

"It's laundry day," she answered.

"It ought to be laundry day every day."

He sat down beside her, hoisted his feet onto the desk, and yawned audibly.

She pushed his feet to the floor and spread out her tutoring folder.

There was a stare-down for a minute or so, then finally he asked, "What are you waiting for?"

"Hell to freeze over," she answered.

"I thought you were here to tutor, Tutor."

"Did you read the passages you were supposed to?"

He snorted and said, "No."

"Listen, Hakiam, let's get one thing straight—"

"I know you're on me, Wendy."

"I'm on you?" she said.

"Yep, you dig me."

She gave a patronizing smile. "I think you have things wrong. I only went out with you because I thought we would have something to talk about, but I was wrong. And if you think that you can just come here and waste time—"

"Like you're so busy with other people."

"It's not my fault that people who have already proven that they can't complete high school in the traditional setting also happen to be the same group of people who have trouble completing their GED in this nontraditional setting. You know the saying, 'You can lead a horse to water but you can't make him drink'—or in this case, think."

He shoved in closer to her and she shoved herself away.

He tipped back in his chair and threaded his hands behind his head.

Wendy went back to paging through her calc book and began to pick up on a weird vibe. She noticed the way he was eyeing her tote bag, which hung on the seat next to her.

"Is there something you want out of my bag?" she asked him.

He wiggled his eyebrows and told her that she better keep a closer eye on her stuff.

"Now, why would I have to worry about that with just you in the room?"

"I'm just saying, don't tempt an honest person."

She took her tote bag and brought it in close to her body. "I won't tempt an honest person *or* you."

He smirked at her remark.

"Don't tell me you're a thief, too, Hakiam?"

He tried to suppress his grin. "All right, I won't tell you," he said.

"Don't you care how you're inconveniencing people?"

"They'll get over it."

"How would you like it if I stole your wallet?"

"There ain't nothing in it. Go to town."

"What if there were something in it?"

"Well, I guess I wouldn't like that."

She gave a perfunctory smile and said, "That's the breakthrough I was looking for."

Then she rose from the chair and stood up tall. "Hakiam, you need to go cold turkey."

"I have. Since I been here in Philly I ain't lifted nothing. Besides, when I did steal back in Cincinnati, I wasn't one of those people who stole just to steal. That's sick."

"You can excuse away anything, Hakiam."

"Just about."

Her nails dug deep in her palm, and she thought hard before she said this next part to him. "Here's an idea. Why don't you get a job?"

"I have a job. I'm a male babysitter."

"No, I mean a paying job. One that earns a steady income, so that you don't have to think about knocking little old ladies over the head for their purses."

He shrugged. "Who the hell would hire me? I don't even have a GED."

Wendy looked Hakiam dead in the eye and said, "This is the United States of America. Trust me, Hakiam, McDonald's is hiring."

17

Even McDonald's wanted references. So did Burger King, KFC, and Long John Silver's. Hakiam found that out the hard way as he traipsed down Chestnut Street and up Market Street, then back down JFK Boulevard. He'd started out pretty early, eleven a.m. (early for him), amid the idled traffic and a smattering of shoppers. The city had a pulse, with its growling buses and honking horns, but every application he took was dead on arrival. They all wanted him to supply the same information, and there was no space on the form to explain that he didn't have a last place worked because he had never worked anywhere formal, and he didn't have anyone to vouch for his character, and he wasn't in any organization that he'd like to mention. So besides his name, Leesa's address, and the fact that he had finished grade school, he didn't have any selling points.

Still, he hit up place after place in a time-murdering exercise called going through the motions.

He collected about seven applications, but he ended up crumpling them all up and tossing them to the wind. He was convinced that all that was going to happen if he did take the time and hand them back in was that he'd be discarded, dumped like shit off a shovel, or worse, left in the bottom of a stack of applications that just got taller and taller.

Why even try?

Hakiam had learned long ago that compassion and understanding were on the list of endangered species. The more you needed something, the less likely you were to get it. So who wanted a job anyway? It was just another hassle. Hakiam would hate having a boss and superiors. They would always check on him. They would come see what he was doing, then they'd walk back. That was what passed for supervision.

If he had a job, he'd hate never quite knowing what he could or couldn't get away with. Should he turn to the window? Should he risk getting lost in thought? Could he take anything from the company refrigerator? Could he take home a stapler or two? Could he borrow that PC for the weekend?

The last place he swung by was a mom-and-pop-style dollar store that actually had a HELP WANTED sign in the window.

It was a cluttered, not-too-clean-looking place. Hakiam had to inch his way in sideways so as not to knock down anything. He asked the lady behind the counter, who had teeth like a beaver, what hours she needed to be covered. She called over her shoulder to someone in the back, "Henry, somebody's out here asking about the job."

The man grunted from behind the curtain, "We don't got any openings. Tell him to hit the road."

His words hovered then settled on Hakiam like dust in the room.

Well, if that doesn't beat all. What kind of rejection was that? At least the man could come out and look Hakiam over before he overlooked him.

Hakiam turned and left with less care than he'd come in with. A box of greeting cards fell on the floor, but he kept moving.

Back outside, he passed more stores, but this go-round he didn't inquire within.

Life just kept stacking up against him. He should have stayed in bed. Nobody was ever going to give him a break, and they had the nerve to call this the City of Brotherly Love. Where was the softness? Where was the compassion? He hated the class distinctions that he saw in Center City. He burned with envy for every rich person who strolled by him. They had their gall, especially the women with their good jobs and their flared trousers with the side zip, their cropped jackets with mandarin collars. Each one of them pecked at the pain, pushing him into deeper anger. There was Hakiam, near-broke, in his bobo sneakers.

Now he was really boxed into a corner. He couldn't steal. He couldn't get a job. What else was there to life?

There was nothing to do but go home to a home that really wasn't his home. Go to his cousin's home and stare at the bumpy warts of ill-plastered walls and the mold spots on the ceiling. That big-eyed girl from the tutoring center was wrong. Real wrong. This wasn't the land of opportunity or milk and honey or gold-paved streets. For him, anywhere he went in America would be the third world.

18

"You lied," he told her as he plopped himself into the chair next to her.

"I did not," she said, barely looking up from her tutoring log. She penciled in the notation: *One student present.*

"Nobody hired me."

She tilted her head to the side. "That doesn't mean I lied."

"You said it would be easy."

"No, I didn't," she told him. "Now you're lying."

"You don't know nothing about nothing."

She grinned. "That shows what you know. That sentence you just used was a double negative, so you essentially said 'I do know something about something'!"

"Well, you don't."

"I was just trying to help you."

He frowned. "Some help."

"All right, then, I won't help. Stay miserable and unemployed and uneducated."

"I tried—"

"Try harder," she interrupted. "Did you try the Gallery?"

"The what?"

"That mall that's downtown by Independence Hall. It has about a hundred stores. Did you try your luck there?"

"I didn't try it at all."

"Well," she said in a leading way.

"Well," he mimicked her.

"Well," she continued, not fazed by his taunting. "I suggest you apply there. Try one of the restaurants."

"Restaurants?"

"I mean, burger joints, pretzel stands, any place where they serve food. You'll never go hungry if you work at a place that serves food."

He met her eyes, and his lip curled.

She sneered back at him.

They shared a few more moments of silence.

He hitched his chin at her. "You want to go out?"

"Out?" she asked.

"Yeah, out."

"Outside?"

"Yeah."

"You want to go out for coffee again?" she asked.

"No." He shook his head. "You want to go out for coffee again?"

Wendy's interior voice always jibed with her exterior one. "No," she said.

He still stared her down. "Feel like coming over my place?"

87

"You have a place?"

"The place I'm staying at."

"What's there?" she asked.

"Me," he said, and when that got no reaction from her, he added, "And Malikia."

Wendy cocked her head to the side and asked, "What's a Malikia?"

"The little girl I watch."

"What's her name again?"

"Malikia," he repeated.

Wendy had never heard that name before, and she mulled it over in her mind. She wondered if it was culturally based or purely fabricated. Moreover, she considered its derivatives. Could it ever be turned into a nickname? "Hi, Mal" or "Good afternoon, Liki." She supposed in a pinch it would go something like this: "Hey there, Maliky."

"You want to see her?" he asked.

Wendy stood up. "I'd love to."

19

Hakiam felt a pang of guilt using a three-month-old as bait to gain back Wendy's interest. But then, he thought, there were worse things he could do. Plus, he wanted to chart her movements once he got her into the ghetto.

Call it a bad joke, but he always thought it was funny to see people out of their natural element. Wendy, as a fish tossed into a different pond, might faint at the smell of garbage or the sight of the urine stains in the corners of the hallways. Or she could trip trying to maneuver past the broken tiles of the flooring. As they hiked up to the third floor, he accidentally kicked a large chunk of peeling gray paint and left a thick black scuff mark in its place. It blended in with the others.

Leesa opened the door. She had on clumsy makeup, a cheap blouse, and spandex bicycle pants. Her chin dropped to the floor when she saw Wendy.

"Hello," Wendy said, holding out her hand. "You must be Hakiam's cousin."

Leesa up-and-downed Wendy and left her extended hand unshaken.

Hakiam ushered Wendy past Leesa into the living room, where Malikia was. Wendy pulled a bottle of hand sanitizer out of her tote bag, murmuring something about guarding against RSV. She rubbed some of the liquid on, then asked to hold the baby. When Leesa shrugged, Wendy stretched out her arms and scooped up the baby.

Malikia took to her magically. It was like a Madonna-and-child reunion. Wendy managed to do more "Itsy Bitsy Spider's" and "Hey, Diddle Diddle's" with Malikia than the little girl had heard in her whole life. Malikia cooed and moved her arms in a herky-jerky motion. Then she snuggled in close to Wendy.

Pretty soon, Hakiam got to feeling like the T in a BLT sandwich: the last of the three. Malikia and Wendy threatened to squeeze him out altogether with their bonding exercises.

He moved to the edge of the room and stood as an onlooker, like his cousin. Leesa clicked her tongue and told Hakiam, "Malikia don't know none of that nursery-rhyme junk. All that's doing is going in one ear and out the other."

Hakiam clucked back at her, "Then it ain't doing no harm."

Leesa picked up her cherry Slurpee and took a gulp.

"She's pretty skinny, Hakiam. I didn't know you liked them like that."

"Who said I liked her?" he asked.

Leesa said, "Nobody."

Hakiam nudged her. "You could offer her something."

"Like what? This is my Slurpee."

"We got water, don't we?"

"*We* ain't got nothing. *I* got some water."

"Well, you gonna stand around being stingy with it? She gave your daughter a onesie. Be a hostess, damnit."

Leesa's face hardened, but she did make a move toward Wendy.

"You want some water?" she asked her.

Wendy was smiling when she said, "No thanks. I'm fine." Then she went back to playing with Malikia.

Hakiam gave Wendy props for staying in the hood past sundown. The evening sky had gone from streaked pink to pitch-black by the time they left the apartment.

"What was that thing you said about ESP?" he asked as he walked her to her car.

"You mean RSV. It's a respiratory tract infection that can be serious in infants born prematurely. It sends thousands of children under two to the hospital each year."

She went on to say that babies like Malikia should always be in a sterile environment and avoid crowds. He thought about the parties Leesa had and wondered if maybe the kid was just naturally immune to this RSV crap. He had certainly never thought to wash his hands before touching Malikia. He always did that afterward.

"You really know your stuff," he told her.

"I've got a lot to learn in order to be a doctor. Even after that there's a lot that's unknowable. Medicine's an art, not a science."

As she reached for the door, he thought, *Okay, it's sink or swim. Now is the time to do it. So start like you mean to finish, Hakiam.*

The streetlights shone down on them, and Leesa, from up above, peered out of a dingy window.

A couple of fellas on the corner twisted around to see.

Here goes nothing. His hand searched up her back, then back down the curve of her spine, and he went in for a landing.

At first, she pushed him away.

He smirked at that. She was a quick one, always with her guard up.

Their eyes met and then she seemed to better understand his intentions. Her defenses melted.

This time she initiated it. She moved her lips closer to his.

They kissed for a few minutes, pressing their bodies together.

20

"You went where?" was her dad's predictable response.

"Fifty-first and Ruby, Dad, and before you MapQuest it, yes, that is square in the slums."

"You're not in the least bit amusing, young lady. I know very well where that is. What did you go there for?"

Wendy told him that she had gone to see the young man she'd been tutoring.

He pointed a stiff finger at her and said, "You're making house calls now? Don't you ever, ever go there again."

It was something Wendy, as the perennial good daughter, had thought she'd never hear. She was actually forbidden to do something! This was cause for celebration, or at the very least a diary entry.

What followed was all new to Wendy. Though her dad had always done a lot of spying on her, this time there was actually substance and not just shadows he was chasing. That Wednesday, he hovered by the doorway of her room after he'd heard her phone go off.

"Is that Erin?" he asked, entering from the hallway.

"Is she the only person I know?" Wendy answered his question with a question.

"It better not be that boy," he warned.

"I've got to go, talk to you later," Wendy told Hakiam, and tried to hang up.

Her father grabbed the phone, saying, "Hello, hello!"

"He's gone, Dad."

"It was him!"

"Dad, you are a genius of detection."

"This has got to stop, Wendy."

"What has got to stop? Me having harmless conversations on the telephone?"

"Yes. I'm canceling this phone."

Wendy sprang to her feet. "What?"

"You don't need it."

"I don't need to communicate with the outside world, Dad?"

"Exactly!" he answered.

"Fine!"

"Wonderful!" he said even louder.

"Fantastic!" she screamed.

With that, her dad exited the room. She thought she was rid of him for the night, but he came back wagging his finger at her. "Let me tell you something else, young lady. Martin Luther King was a great man, but he basically died for nothing when you look at this current crop. His dream of black and white children holding hands—"

"Why are you giving a recitation on black history?"

He continued, "Who in his right mind would want to live next to those people, let alone hold hands with them?"

"You're kind of sweeping through history, aren't you?"

"If I had to live in the ghetto, I'd move."

"Dad, if you had to live in the ghetto, you couldn't move. That's the idea of a ghetto."

He shook his head. "I did move. I grew up on Fifty-first and Kingsessing, and it was a dump back then. I can't imagine what it looks like now. You grew up in the lap of luxury, but I grew up in a fire, Wendy. A fire. I was lucky to make it out of there unscathed. Those mean and nasty people. You don't know what you're getting your-self into."

"Dad, I just talked to Hakiam on the phone. It's not the end of the world."

"Hakiam? What is a Hakiam, anyway? It sounds like a disease. What's the matter with John or Matthew or Thomas?"

"Your name is Thomas."

"Exactly. That's a nice American name."

"Any name can be an American name, Dad."

"Hakiam sounds utterly ridiculous."

"What do you think of Malikia, Dad?" She had to ask.

"That sounds like a disease too. A terminal disease."

"Oh, for God's sake."

"Who's Malikia, anyway? Is that his baby mama?" her father asked.

"He doesn't have any children."

"He doesn't have any children *yet*."

"Well, neither do I."

Her father's eyes became as round as pancakes. "Did you sleep with him?"

21

"What you looking at all those white people for?" Leesa asked, standing squarely in front of the TV with her hands firmly planted on her hips.

He was on the sofa with Malikia underneath his armpit. Hakiam did his best to look around Leesa.

"If it's one thing I hate, it's an old black-and-white movie with nothing but white people in it," Leesa said. "Why are you watching this?"

"Wendy suggested it."

Leesa gave an exaggerated "Ohhhhhhhhhhh," waved her hands in the air in mock fanfare, and went back to blocking his view.

"Will you get out the way? You ain't made of glass," he told her.

She stepped aside for a few moments and asked, "What's it called?"

Hakiam told her he was watching *Twelve Angry Men*.

"What do they got to be so angry about?"

Hakiam didn't answer her.

"What's it about?" she asked.

He sighed. "A jury."

"A jury, huh?" She watched the screen for a few minutes. "Why ain't there any women?"

"I don't know."

"Boy, I hate black-and-white movies with white people. And angry white people, please. That sounds like some bullshit."

"I heard you," Hakiam said, motioning for her to get out of the way.

She held out her hand and said, "I'll get out of the way. You better not have used none of my Netflix."

With his view now unhindered, he got back into the movie. It was at about the twenty-minute mark, and it was really starting to boil. Having been to court a few dozen times, Hakiam was interested to see how things worked on the other end. He always wondered just how those deciders decided. He'd seen them emerge from their back room looking either severe or carefree, but what was the process? Was their debate intense like this movie would have him believe? Or was this all some Hollywood version of reality, and most jurors didn't give a rat's rear? Hakiam guessed the latter but was sucked in all the same.

The movie also played fast and loose with one indisputable fact: courts were never about guilt or innocence; courts were about guilty or not guilty: There was a big difference. That was the fantasy angle of the film, right up there with *X-Men*. Hakiam thought of all the times he'd been taken in for things but couldn't prove he was innocent, versus the times when the charges had been dropped because they didn't have enough evidence to prosecute. In light of that, it was almost comical to see the main character in the movie bring up what-ifs, how-abouts, and suppose-thats left and right just to try to save the poor kid's sorry ass. Real life wasn't like that. People got off on technicalities. People got convicted by momentum.

Leesa came back into the room carrying a bag of potato chips, and Hakiam perked up. "Did you go shopping?" he asked.

Since her mouth was full, she just shook her head no.

"When you do, remember the baby's running low on formula."

"Just water it down, Hakiam. Jesus Christ, what do you want me to do, hold your hand?"

"The can says to use two full scoops."

"You ain't got to listen to the can. Make up your own damn mind. What do I got up in here, one baby or two?"

"Preemies need all the nutrition they can get."

She waved him away.

"Leesa, Wendy said—"

That made Leesa sneer. "Hold up, now I got to take instructions from that skinny thing on nutrition? How many kids she got? What the hell does she know?"

"You're in front of the set again."

"You ain't the least bit into boring shit like that." She grabbed the remote and flicked off the set.

"I am too watching it. Quit being so evil," he said,

grabbing hold of Malikia as he stood up, snatched back the remote, and flicked the set back on.

"I don't know how many times I have to tell you, this is my place and my TV and—"

At that part, Hakiam had heard enough. It was going to drive him mental if he hung around and listened to her anymore. He handed his cousin both the remote control and her daughter.

"Where are you going?" she asked him as she took reluctant hold of Malikia.

"I need air. Bye," he said, and headed out the door to no place in particular.

On his way outside, he passed an open door. The air reeked with drugs. A small, squirrelly-looking guy dressed in a red hoodie and carpenter pants stepped into the hallway and tried to deal Hakiam.

Hakiam kept walking.

Outdoors in the cold night air, he scanned the open sky. He wondered what she was up to right now. Wendy. He was sure whatever she was doing, she didn't have to put up with this kind of crap. He was certain that the only conflict she encountered came from watching actors emote on the screen.

22

Wendy walked cautiously past her father's door. She decided to peek in, and then curiosity got the best of her.

"What's the name of that film, Dad?"

"Quiet" was the answer he first gave her. Then he said, "It's called *Gentleman's Agreement*. It won Best Picture in 1947."

Wendy paused by the doorway, mulling over whether she really wanted to enter the room. She hadn't done that for a while, actually watched a movie with her father.

She eased her way in and sat down by the far wall. Wrapped up in the movie, her dad was at first startled by Wendy. Next, he glanced at her with narrowed eyes; then he went back to watching the TV.

"I bet you've seen this a thousand times," Wendy said.

"Shhh!" he told her.

The premise of the movie was intriguing. A newspaper reporter pretended to be a Jew for eight weeks in order to expose anti-Semitism. Unfortunately, it was during the time period that he was engaged to be married, which gave the movie a compelling subplot. His fiancée was embarrassed to have people think that she was going to marry a Jew. There was also a sophisticated fashion editor who worked at the paper. She wasn't in on the ruse, but she accepted the hero regardless of his supposed religion. Wendy was sure the story would end with the main character leaving his namby-pamby wife-to-be and taking up with the more open-minded, forward-thinking woman. But as the film went on, scene after scene showed the fiancée feeling really, really, really bad about anti-Semitism, but not enough to, you know, stop it. It came to a head when she was at a dinner party and someone told a "kike" joke.

This led to the climax of the film, when the wishy-washy woman had her hand held by a long-suffering Jewish acquaintance. At that point, she was told quite tenderly by this way-too-patient man that she didn't have to go along with bigotry. She could speak up and speak out; she could go against it.

"Can I?" the fiancée said in a warbling voice and with a well-placed tear escaping her eye. "Can I?" she repeated, this time breaking the fourth wall by looking directly into the camera.

"Lame!" Wendy shouted at the TV.

"Will you be quiet?" her father scolded her.

Having lost all hope for the ending, Wendy left the room and went down to the kitchen to get a glass of juice.

Within a few minutes, her father also came downstairs to refresh his teacup.

"That movie was as subtle as a sledgehammer," Wendy told her dad.

"It was made two years after the end of World War Two. People needed a sledgehammer to wake up and see just how wrong prejudice is."

Wendy's chin dropped to the linoleum floor. "Did you just say what I thought you said?"

"I'm not in favor of prejudice, Wendy. I never have been."

Wendy shook her head in almost violent denial. "Dad, hundreds of times I have heard you—"

"You have never heard me speak against Jews. I would never do that. They've been put upon and abused everywhere they go in this world."

"So are *we*."

"We were never rounded up and put in concentration camps, Wendy."

"No, we were rounded up and put on slave ships."

"Still, we were allowed to live."

"So now you're defending slavery, Dad?"

"Slavery isn't genocide, Wendy."

"It may not be genocide, but it's no walk in the park. And what about the Jim Crow laws?"

"Wendy. Wendy. It's ten o'clock at night. This is no time for—"

"I just can't *believe* you, Dad. You have such empathy for one group's struggle and none for our own."

"Jewish people have proven their worth to society. They are intelligent and orderly. They are very well organized."

"What are we, Dad? Chopped liver?"

"It's ten o'clock. I'm going to bed."

Her father added cream to his tea, pouring the last of the carton into his cup, then discarding it.

"Dad, would you object if I applied to Brandeis or Yeshiva?"

"Good night, Wendy."

23

If Hakiam could corner God for twenty seconds, he'd ask him this: *Why are white people always so damn happy?* It didn't seem to matter the day or time: every single moment Hakiam saw a white person, he or she was smiling. His GED teacher was no exception. He stood now at the head of the class, dressed in a V-neck sweater and brown slacks, with a standard-issue grin on his peaches-and-cream face.

His expression didn't match the drabness of the gray room or the lackluster subject matter.

He listed celebrities who never finished high school (Chris Rock, Tom Cruise, and Christina Aguilera, to name a few). He went on to speak with the same optimistic fervor of political figures who were dropouts.

"Former governor Ruth Ann Minner of Delaware left school to support her family, and former senator Ben Nighthorse Campbell dropped out of high school at sixteen to join the air force during the Korean War," he said with a bright grin.

Hakiam stared at the wall to avoid being blinded by the teacher's pearly whites.

Next, the instructor told them that the GED test was split into five parts: reading, writing, mathematics, science, and social studies. Most of it was multiple choice. You could use a calculator but not a dictionary. In the state of Pennsylvania, you could take it over a few days or all at once.

Then the teacher smiled again.

"This is roughly a seven-hour test," he warned, "so pace yourself."

Some students nodded.

Some were lost in space.

Many find school difficult; others find it just plain boring. For Hakiam, GED classes managed to be both at the same time.

Then the teacher talked about how they needed a number 2 pencil and an energy bar for the big day.

"This test is administered every Wednesday at nine a.m. You can take it in English or Spanish. I don't want to give this the hard sell, but you might as well take it now rather than later. You only have eight weeks in this program. Who wants to see where he or she stands? Who would like to sign up for next week?"

Hakiam nodded, absorbing the information, but couldn't bring himself to sign up for the slot. So this whole thing would be over when he just took that test—what was he waiting for? What were any of them waiting for?

He watched as three hands out of thirty went up. One belonged to a dark-complexioned fortyish woman wearing a man's coat and a ski cap. Another was a Hispanic girl who looked young enough to be in high school. The final person was a white girl with a dyed-orange ponytail. She looked to be in her twenties.

Besides that trio, there wasn't a gesture of "sign me up" out of anyone else. The majority of people were as lost in the sauce as he was.

Hakiam felt comforted by this.

24

Their meetings at Wendy's house were clandestine, perfectly synchronized to last until the time that her father came home.

On his first visit, Hakiam gave her house a good once-over. He examined the front porch with its ornamental fretwork. He peered at the three-car garage, which housed only two cars.

Inside, Wendy watched his eyes dart around.

"What, are you casing the joint?" she asked.

He didn't answer at all; he just continued to survey.

"Would you like iced tea, hot tea, soda, juice, water?" Wendy asked him, then smiled slyly. "Or coffee?"

He twisted around to her. "I don't want nothing," he said.

"You must be a camel. They go for days and days without anything to drink."

She led him upstairs to her room, and he ambled

into the walk-in closet to examine himself in the mirror.

"You sure do got everything," he said.

She sat on her bed.

He stretched out beside her.

"The springs on your bed squeak," he announced, as if he were happy to find a flaw.

"I better change the oil," she quipped.

His eyes went back to combing the room.

"This is a real nice setup," he said.

"Thanks," she said, a little embarrassed by the girliness of it, all the stuffed animals and posters that she should have been over already.

He pointed to the cosmetics caddy on her vanity.

"You wear makeup?" he asked.

She nodded.

"It don't look like you do."

"Thank you," she said. "I think."

He brushed her cheek with the back of his hand. "Your skin is real smooth."

She caught his hand with hers and held it to her face. She looked into his large, sensuous eyes surrounded by dark, thick eyelashes—he was one to talk about putting on paint. She'd kill to have her eyes pop like his did.

They kissed for a while.

"So I'm your girlfriend?" she asked.

He was laconic as usual, offering her only a half smile.

"I'm your main squeeze," she proclaimed, pressing

her fingers to her chest, using her stock "soul sister" accent. Then she did a triple snap in the air. It felt freeing to pull it out every now and then. She liked the reaction it got from people. They always looked at her as if to say, *You can do that?*

Hakiam was no exception.

She knew good and well that her usual persona was an uptight priss who always knew the right answers.

"You could be the next Biggie Smalls," he told her.

She knew he was being sarcastic, but still, she decided to up the ante. "Wrong, Hakiam. I could be the next Tupac Shakur."

That made him reel back.

"Hear me out," she told him. "Biggie had the flow but Tupac had the meaning."

He tilted his head to the side as he considered her reasoning.

"Pac it is," he conceded.

She laughed.

"You seem like one of those Tupac fans. They always want to start something," Hakiam said.

"Hey, hey. I thought no one knew what went on that night, either night," Wendy said, feigning innocence. "What did they die, a few months apart? It's a real shame that they escaped the poverty of the streets but not the violence. That's a horrible way to lose someone."

"Yeah." Hakiam gave her a sad look, then brightened into a laugh.

"What's funny?"

"You know, if Tupac had looked like Biggie, he wouldn't have had half his following."

"I don't know. Even without the washboard abs that Tupac had or you have, Biggie did all right with the ladies."

"Yeah, you got that right. I didn't know you knew so much about hip-hop. Who's your favorite rapper that's around now?"

Wendy thought for a while and said, "Britney Spears."

Soon their time was up. While they were getting themselves together, he said, "I almost forgot. I saw your movie."

"My movie?" she asked. "I have a movie?"

"The jawn about the angry dudes."

She ran his words through her mind and tried hard to translate. "Oh," she said finally, "you saw *Twelve Angry Men*?"

"Yeah, I ain't got to the end yet, but you reminded me of the guy who smoked," he told her.

"It was the nineteen-fifties, Hakiam. All the men smoked."

"No, the guy with the glasses," he said.

"A couple of guys had glasses."

"No, the guy who didn't sweat."

"Oh, oh, you mean E.G. Marshall," she said.

"Yeah, he was cool."

Her eyes gleamed. "I'm cool?"

He nodded. "Yeah, under pressure, you don't get emotional."

Wendy frowned; Hakiam really didn't know her at all. If only he were privy to her and her dad's extra-inning volcanic arguments.

Wendy gave him a small smile. "Well, where does emotion get you?"

25

Leesa thumbed through the mail till she got to the letter from the state. "Well, it's about goddamn time," she said.

Hakiam snatched it from her hand and opened it. He scanned its contents quickly. "You get a check to pay for child care?" he asked.

She grabbed it back. "Yeah."

"Well, how come I don't see any of it?"

"Look, for the millionth time, you are living here for free."

"So are you, practically."

"If you don't like the setup here, why don't you hit up your people—"

"You *are* my people," he said.

"Your Cincinnati people."

From the bedroom, Malikia started bawling.

Hakiam spoke over her.

"I want that check."

Leesa clucked her tongue and turned her head.

"Okay, I'll take half of it."

"Dream on, Hakiam."

"I deserve half of it," he insisted.

That made her laugh out loud.

"You're gonna be sorry about this," he warned her.

"Yeah, yeah," she said.

He felt like taking her throat into a vise grip. He wanted so badly to strangle her till her last breath. Instead, he chose to sting her with words. "You are one greedy bitch."

"Well, maybe that uppity girl you see will treat you better."

"Leave her out of it. She's way better than you. At least she's not cheap and petty like you are."

Leesa laughed again. "She cares even less about you than I do. And let me tell you something, Hakiam, that's saying something."

Hakiam held up his hand to halt her words.

Leesa kept right on talking. "I tell you why she's going out with you. She's curious. She just wants to see how the other half lives. You're a science experiment to her."

Broiling, he let his cousin keep talking just to see where she would go. "Is that right?" he asked.

"Yeah, that's right. She's not interested in Malikia, and she sure as hell ain't interested in you."

"You know everything, Leesa."

She nodded and stuffed the check back into its envelope. "How could she be, Hakiam? You ain't her kind.

You ain't going nowhere. You ain't about nothing. She can't take you around Mommy and Daddy. Beyond satisfying her curiosity, you're worthless to her."

That was taking it too far. Hakiam wondered if Leesa realized the irony in what she was saying. She had said all this staring at him like he was a germ or something under a microscope, and she had room to criticize Wendy? Where did she get off?

For the second time in a very short while, Hakiam stormed out of Leesa's apartment.

"Where are you going?" Leesa called after him.

"Away from you."

26

The seasonal display was kicking in at the mall, a giant leap from Halloween straight to Santa.

Hakiam and Wendy sat at a wrought-iron table in the mall's atrium; Wendy was singing the alphabet for Malikia's benefit. Malikia was in the drooling stage, still moving in herky-jerky motions. Hakiam bopped his head, following along with the singsongy beat.

"You follow along pretty well," Wendy complimented Malikia and turned to Hakiam. "And so do you."

Hakiam's customary scowl melted to a half smile.

Malikia tugged on Wendy's blouse.

"That means she wants to hear it again," Hakiam told Wendy. "She don't get much of this entertainment at home."

"*A, B, C, D,*" Wendy began singing, then said, "You know, there are tapes at the library that you can get." Her eye went back to Malikia. "*E, F, G.*" She told Hakiam, "That would help her—"

"Her mother ain't into all that." Hakiam broke into *"H, I, J, K,"* then went back to "She ain't gonna bother with that."

"L, M, N, O, P," Wendy began, then switched to "Well then, why don't you pick up the ball and—"

"I need to find a new place." He winked at Malikia. *"Q, R, S, T, U, V,"* he sang. "To live."

"How will she get by without you?" Wendy asked. Then she turned back to Malikia. *"W, X—"*

"Y do you care?" Hakiam broke in. "She's all set up," he said. *"Z."*

"Well, that can't last forever," Wendy said.

"If she has more Malikias it will."

Wendy gave an I'm-going-to-gobble-you-up look to Malikia and then said, "She's a cutie, but that's one heck of a plan."

"Yeah, women have it made."

"Hold on, Hakiam. It takes a man and a woman to do that."

"Whatever."

"You said Leesa works outside the home."

"Part-time."

"Hakiam, you don't even do that."

"Look, Wendy, let's go back to the ABCs."

"It sounds like you need to make other living arrangements. I mean, you can't keep . . . " Wendy's voice trailed off as her throat constricted. Out of the corner of her eye, she caught sight of them: Rhea, Jillian, and Carlyle.

Why were they always here? Since when was this their domicile?

117

"Oh, shit," Wendy said.

Malikia smiled.

Wendy grimaced. She definitely didn't want to teach the baby that word.

Hakiam twisted around to see what she was looking at.

"It's them," she said.

"Who?"

Wendy took the baby off her lap and handed her over to Hakiam. She stood and threw back her shoulders. Unlike the last time she'd run into these girls, she was free from the constraint of her father.

She walked over to them. "Don't even think of messing with me. Go back to your other hobby—shopping or shoplifting or however you were occupying your time before you saw me."

"What does she mean by that?" Rhea asked, feigning innocence and elbowing her clique members.

Carlyle and Jillian gave looks of exaggerated surprised that went well with their teenybopper Limited apparel.

"You know exactly what I mean—leave me alone."

With their two-faced smiles, high ponytails, and jiggling charm bracelets, they were going to say something stupid. Wendy knew it. They didn't disappoint.

"Is that your baby daddy?" Rhea asked.

Carlyle and Jillian laughed on cue.

Wendy's blood beat hot. Her internal voice sought to jibe with her exterior voice, but she couldn't think of a darn thing to say. She found herself wishing she could just deck their cutely made-up faces.

She pointed at them. "Just keep away."

Wendy turned and left them right where they stood. She went back to Hakiam and Malikia and tried to put the girls out of her mind by reapplying her beige lipstick.

But the trio couldn't leave well enough alone. Though they kept their distance, they continued pointing and giggling and playing Wendy for sport.

"Are those white chicks trying to mess with you?" Hakiam asked her.

He didn't wait for her to answer.

"I never liked bullies," he said.

Wendy watched him spring into action. He placed Malikia in her lap. He rolled up on the three of them, and they seemed to physically shrink about a foot each. The ceiling seemed to compress on them. He spoke to them for only a few minutes but came back to the table in a strut.

"What did you say?" Wendy asked him.

Hakiam gave her one of those playful chucks to the chin, then leaned back into his chair. "I told them if they didn't leave you alone I was going to do a drive-by."

"A *drive-by*?" Her eyebrows perked up. "You don't even have a car."

Wendy shot a glance back their way. Jillian, Carlyle, and Rhea looked decidedly meek and tamed.

The next thing that happened really seemed like science fiction to Wendy. They scraped their way over with humbled and bowed heads, and Rhea did the impossible. She said these words: "We're sorry for messing with you."

Wendy could only imagine what fear prickled their minds when they were face to face with someone they couldn't bully. She couldn't help a slow smile from lifting the edges of her mouth. They had *apologized* to her. Where was Perez Hilton when you needed him? This gossip belonged on his blog.

That evening, Wendy couldn't wait to punch Erin's number into her cell. She recounted the events for her best friend with relish.

"That's just what I always suspected about them— they can dish it out but they can't take it."

"He really shook them. You should have seen the look on their faces."

"Well, they are really sheltered girls. I bet they mistake Justin Timberlake for Timbaland."

27

The limp green leaves on the ground mixed with the cornflake texture of the brown ones as Hakiam, Wendy, and Malikia breathed in the crisp late-autumn air of Fairmount Park. They were getting to be the Three Musketeers, always in each other's company.

That Saturday, Wendy was dragging along a picnic basket so big she was lopsided with it. Hakiam had a peaceful and content Malikia on his shoulders.

Suddenly a bike rider stopped in front of them and jammed his hand down the back of his shorts, fishing and fishing. This went on for quite a while, like he had a mega-wedgie.

Wendy turned her head, and Hakiam pulled her and Malikia down under an umbrella of trees. After a blanket was spread out, Hakiam and Wendy enjoyed tuna fish sandwiches as Malikia feasted on pureed apricots.

Hakiam was in awe of Wendy. She did it so well: the

patting and whispering as she spooned out that orange glop to Malikia.

"People this age are perfect," Wendy told him. "It takes next to nothing to make them happy. All they want is some hugs and silly songs and they're set—what's not to love?"

"Do you want your own baby?"

They looked out at the Schuylkill River as they ate.

"Yes," she answered eagerly, then qualified, "when I'm thirty-two."

"Thirty-two is old. Why do you want to wait that long?"

"Thirty-two is nothing anymore. People are living into their eighties. By then, I'll be out of medical school and three years into my practice."

"I could see you with a little girl."

There was a chill in the air but the sky was powder blue.

"I could see you with a boy, Hakiam," Wendy mused aloud. "A bunch of boys. A whole football team."

Hakiam turned away. "I don't think I'll have any kids."

"Why not?"

"I don't got nothing to offer. I don't think I'll ever be situated."

"Ever?" Wendy asked.

"Nope."

"Forever's a long time, Hakiam."

They did more strolling and talking, then they put the leftovers back in Wendy's car. They walked out of the park into the neighborhood, where an old man was sitting on the cement stoop of a storefront with his hands out, saying, "You don't have to be a Rockefeller to help a fella."

Wendy handed him a buck, then they went back to her car and put an already sleeping Malikia in her car seat.

Hakiam jerked his thumb in the old man's direction. "I'll probably end up like that guy."

"Don't say that," Wendy said.

"It's true."

"Do you know tomorrow?"

"No, but I know today. I can't go back and I can't go forward."

"You sound like Bigger Thomas."

"Hold up, since when do you use that word?"

"What? Oh, I said *Bigger* Thomas, a character in a book. I don't use that other word."

"Why not?"

"Why? What purpose does the word 'nigger' serve, besides to transmit hate?"

"You can't take that word away from us now. And you don't have to say it in hate."

Wendy held up her hand. "We're not going to agree on that. I don't get any love from that word."

"Well, of course not, look at where you're from."

"Oh, not that again."

"Yeah, that again." He paused. "Tell me about the dude."

"What dude?"

"The dude from the book."

"Oh, the book's called *Native Son*. What you said before reminded me of a line toward the end: 'I had to kill because you wouldn't let me live.'"

"Yeah, it gets like that sometimes."

"You're not in the same predicament that that character was."

"How can you be so sure?"

"He killed a white girl and stuffed her into the furnace."

"Say what?"

"It's a classic, Hakiam. Read it yourself if you don't believe me."

"I'll take your word for it."

She started up the engine, but she could tell he was still thinking of the plot of the novel.

"You're right, Wendy, things could be worse," he said.

"These are just things left over from our outing," Wendy told Leesa after they got to her place. "Do you mind if I put them in the fridge?"

Leesa folded her arms across her chest and shot her a hostile look.

Wendy deposited the extra bread and cheese and sparkling water on the kitchen table. "I'll leave these right there."

Hakiam stood holding Malikia and biting his tongue. Why did his cousin have to be so rude?

Wendy kissed Malikia's hand and waved goodbye. "See you, sweetie."

Hakiam put Malikia in Leesa's arms and told Wendy, "I'll walk you to your car."

When Hakiam came back, Leesa had relegated the baby back to her crib and still had an evil look on her face.

"I don't want you to take Malikia out again."

Hakiam stepped back. "Oh, really?"

"I don't ever want—"

He held up his hand. "Yeah, yeah."

"Well, you better do what I say. I don't want that girl around my daughter anymore."

"Why?"

"I ain't got to give you a why, just do it."

He nodded knowingly at Leesa's naked jealousy and did an exaggerated salute. "Yes, sir."

28

The next time they went out, Hakiam and Wendy wandered about all afternoon until the combination of hunger and frugality drew him to a sandwich board. It promised shrimp for $2.99.

"You like shrimp?" he asked.

"Who doesn't?" she answered.

Unlike that coffee shop where the fragrance of cinnamon and vanilla swirled in the atmosphere, in this place, the odor of frying grease hung in the air. It was stuffy and crowded.

"How many shrimp do you get?" Hakiam asked the man at the register.

"About ten. No, maybe twenty."

"Twenty shrimp for two-ninety-nine?" Wendy asked.

"Yep," the man said.

Hakiam held up two fingers, signaling that he'd take two orders.

Wendy stopped him, saying that if there were twenty, why didn't they just split it.

"Would you like to make it a combo for just a dollar more?" the guy at the counter asked.

Hakiam thought of his stash, now down to forty-something dollars. That was all he had to his name.

"You want to combo it?" the guy repeated.

A nearly grown man trying to take a girl out with a pathetic $43, eating $2.99 shrimp.

"No," he said.

He handed the man three of his forty-three dollars.

"It'll be a little more than that," the guy said. "You're downtown. Seven percent sales tax."

Before he could dig back into his funds, Wendy shoved a twenty at him and then flipped a quarter at the cashier.

"I can't take money from you," Hakiam said.

"Why not?"

"Where I'm from men pay the way."

"Where are you from, 1957?"

The cashier smirked at that.

When their order came up, they took it to a booth. Hakiam reached for a shrimp. It was hot. Not spicy hot, asbestos-glove-needing hot.

Wendy squinted at the food and noticed something. "These shrimp aren't deveined," she said as she dug into one, taking off the breading, only to get black waste material under her fingernails.

"What does that mean?" he asked.

"It means these shrimp are laced with crap!" she exclaimed.

"You're bourgie, you let a little dookie scare you," Hakiam said as he rooted in the bag for another shrimp.

She grabbed a napkin to clean her hands. "Maybe we should take this back."

Hakiam finished that shrimp and reached for another. "What's the big deal? It's natural."

"You're going to sit there and defend shit?"

"I guess you feel too good to eat this."

She nodded. "Yes, I'm too good to eat shit, Hakiam. Yes, I am."

As they argued, Hakiam kept right on eating. Her contrary words didn't spoil his appetite. If there was food in front of him, he couldn't let it go to waste.

He balled up the wrapper and they left.

The sky had changed from a dull gray to a sunny yellow, but they were still storming at each other.

"Make sure you never take Malikia to a place like that. She's liable to get Listeria."

"She could get what now?" Hakiam asked.

"Listeria. There are one hundred known cases a year. It's a foodborne illness and the effects—"

"I'll take your word for it, Wendy."

"Be sure you tell her mother about that."

"Her mom won't listen to you. She doesn't even want you taking Malikia places anymore."

Wendy's eyebrows knitted together. "Me? What did I do? I've been very nice to that little girl."

"That's the point."

"What's the point?"

"Nothing," Hakiam all but grunted. "Look, let's just change the subject."

"No, let's stay on this subject. Your cousin is using that sweet little baby as a pawn. She doesn't really think that I would ever try to hurt her daughter, does she?"

"Let's just change the subject."

"I don't see why she would forbid me to see Malikia. What was the reason she gave?"

"You're like a dog with a bone, Wendy. Let it go. Look, you and Leesa are pretty far apart—"

"Well, so are you and I. So are every single person in the world and everybody else."

"It's not that simple."

"Yes, it is. She's trying to make it so complex, but all it boils down to is that someone cares for her daughter and she doesn't like it. What sense does that make? If I were a single mother, I'd take help from wherever I could get it!"

"She gets help. She don't have to pay for hardly anything."

"Well, the government won't give her kid a hug," Wendy said.

Hakiam had no comment on that, and the conversation stalled. They were on Twenty-second Street, near where she had parked her car. She glanced down at her watch and made an excuse to escape.

"I better go," she said. "I've got things to do at home."

"What things?"

"College applications." She blurted out the first thing that came into her mind.

"Where are you applying?" he asked.

She sighed. She really didn't want to start up a new conversation. "Lately, I've been looking at Howard."

He stopped in his tracks. "You want to go to a black school?" There was more than a trace of horror in his voice.

She threw her shoulders back and squared off with him. "Yes," she said.

"Wendy, you know what people say about black colleges."

"The blacker the college, the greater the knowledge," Wendy said, telling Hakiam what she had seen on a T-shirt once.

"No, people will think you went there because you couldn't get in no place else."

"Is that what you think?"

"That's what people would think."

She searched his face. "Hakiam, I'm asking, what do *you* think?"

He'd been blunt up to this point and didn't stop there. "Well, I know one thing: I wouldn't be going to no black school if was smart like you."

29

"It's like I'm dating my dad, Erin."

"I think that's illegal in Pennsylvania."

Wendy and Erin veered into a coffee shop on the corner of Sixteenth and Walnut Street. They stood at the counter and studied the menu for a few moments.

Wendy ordered a mocha, and Erin had a chai. They split a strawberry scone.

"I'm between two fires. I get burned whether I choose Hakiam or my dad."

"Maybe you should give him another chance," Erin said, brushing her shoulder-length golden hair away from her collar.

"Which him?"

"Both."

"How can I do that? They're at opposite ends of the spectrum." Wendy drank her mocha. "But then they aren't. Why are both of them against black colleges?"

Erin shrugged. "Maybe they're both uninformed. You

said your dad grew up poor, and Hakiam is poor. They may have more in common than you think."

Wendy found herself wishing she had never met Hakiam. Why did she have to volunteer at that community center in the first place? Instead of tutoring, she could have learned a new language. Greek or Arabic. German or Mandarin. Anything.

"You know, on paper this is supposed to work out. How many times have you heard that opposites attract: Mr. Wild and Crazy meets Miss Predictable and Boring?"

Erin patted her hand. "You're not boring, Wendy."

"You're lucky, Erin. You and Kyle. You two can date and it doesn't turn into sociology class. I'm stuck."

"No, you're not. You can date anyone you want."

Wendy laughed out loud. "Everything I do is a statement. If I date a poor black guy, that means something; if I date a well-off black guy, that means something; if I date a white guy—"

"You can date whoever you want. Nobody but ignorant people think that way."

"I just can't go out with a guy or pick a school. Whatever I choose to wear or say, I'm either a sellout or a militant."

"You're Wendy Anderson. End of story."

Wendy twirled her finger in the air, feigning being impressed. "I'm Wendy Anderson—whoopee!"

"Just be yourself," Erin said, her light blue eyes boring into Wendy's brown ones. "That's good enough for me."

Wendy smiled at her friend.

Erin winked at her. "Now, as for Hakiam. You should take out a piece of paper and put on one side what you like about him and on the other side what you don't."

"What's that going to do?"

"It will give you an inventory. You really need to sort things out with him."

"I don't know, Erin. I don't know if that'll help or not."

"Well, why don't you let me meet him? It'll be fun, plus I want to meet him. And you owe me a double date."

With that, Wendy agreed, figuring she might as well enjoy having a boyfriend while she had one.

30

Wendy could run, but she couldn't hide. No matter how badly he pissed her off, Hakiam was bound to see her at the tutoring center.

He went up to where she was seated and tapped her chair. "What you reading about?"

She put down her psychology book, marking her place with a pen. "I have a Freud test next week. But I really think he's outdated now. All that mumbo jumbo about the id and the superego. And don't get me started on all his mother issues."

Hakiam pulled up a chair. "I got mother issues."

Wendy put her hand under her chin. "Do tell?"

"My mom was selfish. Everything good was for her. She used to hide all the Frosted Flakes in her bedroom. She left the no-name shit in the kitchen for us."

Wendy laughed out loud. "I'm sorry, Hakiam, but I outgrew Tony the Tiger by the time I was ten."

"She was evil and stingy. She never gave us anything nice to eat or to wear. Everything was for her, her, her. She didn't give a damn about my sisters and me."

"Sisters? You have sisters?"

"I had five. Now I got four."

"What happened?" Wendy asked.

"Adasida got shot. She was getting her hair braided. It was a stray bullet. It came through the window."

"Oh, my God," she said. "That's horrible, Hakiam."

"Yeah."

"How old was she?"

His eyes flickered with anger, then went back to blank, dense sadness. "Twelve. She was my second-oldest sister."

Wendy lowered her head and shook it.

"After that, my mom started farming us out."

She looked up at him. "What does that mean?"

"She split us up. That was about the same time she caught my oldest sister, Rashida, in bed with this guy down the block. He was forty. My mom said it was too much for her to handle with us getting out of control."

"That doesn't make any sense. It seems like she would want to keep her family close after a tragedy like that, not push them away. And your mom should have reported that jerk down the block to the police. If Rashida was under eighteen, what he did was statutory rape," she told him. "People like that should be locked away. No wonder you left Cincinnati, Hakiam."

"A lot of bad things happened to me in my life, that's

just a couple of them," he said matter-of-factly, with that same desperate stare from hollow eyes. "Besides, that happened eight years ago. There's not a damn thing you can do about it now."

Wendy nodded, not so much to say she agreed as to say she understood. There was so much she wanted to say to Hakiam, but it all came out as silence.

And more silence.

"Why did your mom let you move here?" Wendy finally asked.

"She ain't have no say about it. I moved out on my own."

"You mean you ran away?" Wendy asked.

Hakiam's face was closed. "No, I just left."

"Why would your mother—"

"I aged out," Hakiam said.

"You're talking about foster care, aren't you?" Wendy asked Hakiam.

He nodded.

"Well, what in the hell were you doing there? Where was your mother and how could you age out? You're still under eighteen!"

"I only had a year to go," Hakiam said. "I didn't want to wait till the last minute."

"I just don't understand your mom," Wendy said. "Where was she during all this? Did she just walk away from all of you?"

"She put us in the system. You can do that—if you're tired of raising kids, you can give them to the state."

"That shouldn't be allowed. If you're a parent, that's not like a part-time job. You can't just walk anytime you want. That's insane."

Wendy noted now that Hakiam's eyes showed no recognizable sign of feeling.

"So, what's foster care like?" she asked.

"You're the smart one, Wendy. What do you think foster care is like?"

Her eyebrows slid upward as she said, "That bad, huh?" She stood up and walked over to the water cooler. She brought back two cups and handed him one.

"You've really been through it," Wendy said, then tossed her head back and drank her water in one swallow.

He did the same.

They sat facing each other and she took his hand, but after a while he removed her hand from on top of his.

Then he pulled out his American history textbook and began to read.

Not to be outdone, she opened up her psych book again, shutting him out from view but not from thought.

After twenty minutes of feigned concentration, he began to get restless and drummed his fingers on the table.

She reached out to still his hand. She cocked one eyebrow. "You free Saturday?"

He nodded.

"Ever been on a double date?"

He shook his head.

"We shouldn't have to sneak around. You mind meeting my father before we go?"

He shrugged.

She held out her hand for him to shake. He brought her in for a kiss instead.

31

"Hakiam's downstairs."

"And?" her father asked, already in his pajamas and bathrobe at just past seven.

"Aren't you coming down to meet him?"

"Why should I? I'm familiar with his type."

"That's rude."

"I'm allowed to be rude, I'm your father. Pass me the *TV Guide*."

"As if you don't already know what's on television every minute of every day," she said, but handed him the magazine.

"Thank you," he said, and paged through till he got to the right day and time.

"Oh, good," he said. "Cary Grant is on. Now, he was someone with real class."

Wendy rolled her eyes.

Her dad clicked on the television. "I have tried my whole life to escape people like Hakiam, and you have the unmitigated gall to bring someone like that right into this house." He took a sip of his tea and told her, "You cannot lift him up. He can only drag you down."

Wendy turned to leave.

"I hope that you didn't expect me to support this thug crush."

"What I expected of you was that you try to understand me for once."

"I always listen to you, Wendy. He seems to delight in giving SparkNote versions of how bad his life is."

"No, you don't, Dad. You don't listen and you don't even try to understand. You just sit in this room every night and watch old movies. Well, I want to relate to people, not a TV set."

"Wendy, I have done my best to put you in a nice neighborhood, and what do you do?"

"Hakiam has never pulled me away from you. There is no one pulling me away from you besides *you*, Dad." She paused. "You made it out of the slums—why don't you have any faith that someone else can too? Why are you so anxious to slam the door behind you?"

"It's because I slammed the door that I was able to make it out. But you can't see that. Because comfort is all you've known."

"There's all different types of comfort, Dad."

"Look, I'm not going to continue to go round and round. Respect these gray hairs on my head, young lady," he said, pulling at his salt-and-pepper hair.

"You're impossible, Dad."

"That may be true," he said, looking over the top of his glasses at her. "Erin's meeting you there?"

"Yes, Dad."

"Well, be sure to come straight home afterward."

"Yes, Dad."

She went back downstairs. Hakiam was right where she'd left him, sitting in a big chair, staring at nothing in particular. She was expecting him to at least have a so-I-guess-he-ain't-coming-down look on his face. Instead, he wore no expression whatsoever. Right by him on the breakfront was the family photo of her, her mom, and her dad when they were one small happy family. Hakiam didn't even seem interested in that.

She got her blue wool coat from the hall closet, and they left.

When they got outside, Wendy felt compelled to say, "I'm sorry my dad is like that."

"Do I look like the type that's dying to meet the folks?"

"I wanted him to meet you, Hakiam. I wanted him to give you a chance."

"Look, I just said I ain't into parents no way. I'm not even bothered with my own father. Why should I get mixed up with yours?"

"I don't know. Maybe because I would like you to?"

"Well, he don't want to, so why don't you let it drop."

Wendy took a deep breath. "I don't think it's too much to ask, Hakiam, for you and him to spend five minutes face to face being civil to one another like two normal human beings."

"Ain't it bad enough that I got to spend time with your white friends?"

"Why do they have to be my *white* friends?"

"Because that's what color they are."

"They have names, you know," Wendy said in a decidedly short tone.

She could tell that her words had struck Hakiam like a lash. "Sorry," he said after a pause.

She walked ahead of him as they went to the car.

"You look nice tonight," he said.

She glanced down at her V-neck cardigan, square-necked camisole, and blue jeans.

"Thanks," she told him over her shoulder.

They arrived at the busy IHOP at eight o'clock sharp. Erin and Kyle had already secured a table, and Erin waved wildly at the sight of her friend. Both she and Kyle rose to greet Wendy and Hakiam.

Kyle was medium height with well-scrubbed looks. He dressed like a jock, though he never played varsity ball.

Though originally from Jersey, Erin suffered from that middle-America openness.

Hakiam acknowledged them both with a nod, and they all sat down.

They all flipped the menu over from the dinner portions to the breakfast selections and ordered various incarnations of pancakes.

"How do you like it here in Philadelphia?" Erin asked, her head bobbing in her attempt to be friendly.

Wendy cringed. She knew Hakiam would be immune to Erin's sunny nature. He'd do just like John F. Kennedy had said and mistake her kindness for weakness.

Hakiam shrugged. "It's about the same. A city's a city."

"Well, not every place has the Liberty Bell," Erin said with a bright smile.

"What's Cincinnati like?" Kyle asked.

"Isn't the Rock and Roll Hall of Fame there?" Erin asked.

Hakiam gave Wendy an I'm-lost look.

Wendy winked at him. "That's Cleveland," she said. "And the funny thing is, whenever there's a new inductee into the Hall of Fame, they hold the ceremony in New York."

"Well, you can't expect the Stones to go to Ohio," Kyle said.

Erin nodded. "This country consists of New York and LA. Everything else is flyover territory."

"Don't say that. I just sent off my application to Notre Dame," Kyle said

"Where's that?" Hakiam asked.

"Indiana," Erin said. She poured a touch of maple syrup on her silver-dollar banana pancakes.

"Colleges don't count," Wendy said. "Most campuses are a world within themselves."

Kyle sliced up his blueberry pancakes. "I think it's so cool that you're getting your GED, Hakiam. Have you thought at all about college?"

Hakiam forked a hunk of buttermilk pancakes into his mouth and said, "Nope."

"The program lasts another few weeks," Wendy said.

"What are your plans after it's over?" Kyle asked.

Hakiam shrugged. "I'll see if I pass."

"Oh, you'll pass," Wendy said confidently. "I've never had a tutee fail yet."

"Wendy, you said you never had a tutee take the test," Erin said.

Wendy gently kicked her under the table. "That was supposed to be our secret."

Hakiam laughed and said, "I knew I was in good hands."

As they finished their meal, Kyle tossed out the following question: "I know a guy who's throwing a party—you want to hit that?"

"Sure," Hakiam said, "let's hit that."

When they entered the party, Wendy fiddled with the buttons on her jacket. She was reluctant to take it off. Wendy was missing the teen gene: she hated parties and already missed the good time they'd been having simply sitting around talking and eating carbs. Parties were loud and crowded and featured flat beer that came in red plastic cups. The air reeked of drugs, and there was no room to move or think.

At the gathering, there were a few kids she knew from school. They were grinding on the makeshift dance floor or lounging on the lumpy brown couch.

"Hey, that's Jay-Z playing," Hakiam said.

Wendy turned to Hakiam and asked, "What were you expecting, a hoedown?"

He pointed to two girls at the center of things making out with each other.

"I see some hos."

Kyle laughed so hard that he spit out his drink.

Erin giggled too and elbowed Wendy. "Come on, that was funny. You know they're just going at each other to attract guys' attention."

Wendy sighed and played Hakiam's comment over again in her head. A grin crept over her face.

As the party went on, Wendy felt her mind and body becoming connected with the silly atmosphere. She knew her dad was going to ream her no matter what time she came back, so she figured she might as well go for broke and break her curfew.

She took the banana clip from her hair and started dancing, working all angles. She threw her hands in the air and spun around with Hakiam, then Kyle, then Erin, then went back to Hakiam again. They mingled and mixed it up with the rest of the crowd and stayed till the party was broken up around one (thanks to an angry neighbor who claimed he had to get up early the next morning).

As they left, Hakiam told Wendy, "Hey, white people are all right!"

"You know," Kyle said, "that would make a good bumper sticker."

32

It was past one, and every inch of the apartment was filled with bodies. Leesa's friends were sitting on folding chairs, kitchen chairs, dining room chairs, stools, and the plastic-covered sofa. One friend, Rashana, kept circulating with a plate of this or a pitcher of that.

And that *music*. The wild beat kept going and going till the room seemed to swirl with absolute chaos. New people were still entering the apartment, closing in on Hakiam.

"What happened on your hot date tonight? Did that stuck-up girl finally give you some?" Leesa asked at first sight of him.

"Never mind all that," Hakiam told her. "It looks like you got half of Philly up in here."

She raised her glass. "That's right and we're gonna get a high high."

Hakiam pushed past his cousin and threaded through the crowd. He was stopped by an older woman. She appeared to be in her thirties or maybe forties and was dressed like a walking Lava Lamp, in a yellow dress and gold wig.

"What's your sign?" she asked Hakiam, throwing an arm around him.

"Closed," he said, tossing her arm back.

A touch of the goodwill from his outing with Wendy and her friends still remained, but after a few minutes at his cousin's, he felt the usual tension returning. His neck joints felt tight. There were bottles and cans everywhere, but he didn't want to drink to make himself feel loose. He wanted to sleep.

He went to the bedroom in the hope of lying down. Instead, he got the shock of his life. There was Malikia, all nineteen inches of her.

She had rolled off the bed onto the floor and was out cold.

And she was lying in a drying pool of blood.

33

In the thin predawn night, Wendy walked up to her front door. Her dad opened it as she was fumbling with the keys.

He stood above her like a prison warden.

Then he let her in, not saying a word, and Wendy made her way upstairs.

In her room, she changed into shorts and a T-shirt and got into bed. She was still wound up from the night, so she tried to burn off some energy by squaring her nails with a file.

Her cell buzzed: Hakiam. It had only been fifty minutes since she'd dropped him off at his front door.

When she answered, he didn't waste any time. "Malikia fell off the bed. She's not moving," he told her.

Wendy threw off the covers. "Call nine-one-one," she said.

"I did that."

Just then, her father came in, saying, "Get off the phone. Call that person back tomorrow."

Wendy waved at him to go away.

"Wendy, who is that?" her father asked. "Is that that boy? You just spent the evening with him. Hang up."

"Call nine-one-one again," Wendy told Hakiam. "Tell them it's a baby. Tell them it's an infant. Then call me back."

Hakiam said he would and clicked off.

"It's late at night. What do you think you're doing?" her dad said.

"There is an emergency!"

"What kind of emergency? What are you talking about?"

Wendy stepped into her jeans and pulled a sweatshirt over her head.

"Wendy, you are not leaving this house. I forbid you. There is always an emergency with those people. They will have you running from crisis to crisis."

"Come on, Dad. For God's sake, why do you have to start up with this shit now?"

"And I would trust that you know to speak to me better in this house!"

"A baby is unconscious, Dad. She could die!"

The cell went off again. She grabbed it and answered, and Hakiam shouted over the music pounding heavy in the background.

"Hakiam, who's there with you?"

"Plenty of people. It's a party."

"Ask if anyone knows first aid," Wendy said.

"He needs to get the baby to a doctor," Wendy's dad said.

"Ain't nobody here knows nothing," Hakiam said when he got back on the line.

"Why hasn't the ambulance come yet? Call them again," Wendy told him.

She heard him step away, and then the faint sound of a siren. She breathed deeply, then asked when he came back to the phone, "Is the ambulance there?"

"No, that's gone on down the street," Hakiam said.

"You're going to have to get her to a hospital."

"What's the nearest one?"

She shot a look at her father.

"What's the nearest hospital to Fifty-first and Ruby?"

He paused a moment, then said, "Misericordia."

"What is it on?"

He frowned. "It's on Fifty-fourth Street."

Wendy told Hakiam, "Keep her as still as you can, but get her to Misericordia on Fifty-fourth Street."

34

Hakiam had never thought of himself as a runner, but he had been known to book it when the time called for it. And he did have some experience running with items in tow. Still, he never thought he'd have to tear down city streets with an infant tucked up tight in his arms.

He had stripped a sheet from the bed and thrown it around Malikia before bolting out the front door. His sneakered feet thumped against the cement and he pitched forward as his cousin trailed him with cries of, "Hakiam, this is your fault!"

His long legs and arms moved smoothly as he poured himself like liquid through the night.

When the hospital finally came into sight, he pushed harder. By the time he got there, his lungs were burning and his limbs spasming.

He set a still-limp and unresponsive Malikia on the ER check-in counter. He must have said something, must have answered some questions, but it passed in a blur. In what seemed like mere seconds, Malikia was whisked away on a small gurney. Masked men and women took her off in a whirl of beeps and monitors, similar to the way she had come into the world.

Then Leesa came through the door, panting and crying. She followed the medical team into the curtained room where Malikia had been taken.

Hakiam was about to follow her when the lady behind the desk handed him a slew of papers, saying, "She'll be well taken care of. We'll do the best we can. Please fill these out."

He made his way to the corner of the room.

Hakiam paged through the forms, unable to focus. His cell went off and he put it to his ear.

"I'm just past Lancaster Avenue. Are you still at the apartment?" Wendy asked.

"I'm at the hospital."

"Did the ambulance ever come?"

He caught his breath. "No."

"What part of the hospital are you in, pediatric intensive care or the emergency room?"

He told her and she clicked off.

He had a headache. His body was weary from the run. He closed his eyes, hoping to wake up from this bad dream.

With the music going so loud, he hadn't heard the thump. But then again, he had only been there for a few moments. The blood was dry. She might have been lying there for hours before he found her.

Hakiam kept going through things in his head. How could this be? Malikia had never fallen before.

Leesa came back into the lobby area. Hakiam's red eyes met hers.

"What's going on?" Hakiam asked her.

"They kicked me out."

"What are they doing?"

"Prepping for surgery."

"Oh, shit," Hakiam said, throwing down the paperwork.

Leesa pointed at him. "It was you. You're the one who was supposed to be responsible for her."

"I wasn't even there."

"Exactly, Hakiam. And you should have been."

The rotating blue light flashed on an ambulance outside. Another emergency patient was wheeled in. Doctors, nurses, and aides flanked the gurney as it was hustled through the door and down the corridor. Behind all that bustle, Hakiam saw Wendy and her father come in.

Wendy ran right up to Hakiam and embraced him. As Hakiam held her, his eye caught the disgusted look of her father, who seemed to be saying, *I'm glad I didn't come downstairs to greet you. You are* exactly *what I expected.*

Then Leesa started up. "Why did you call her?" she said. Her voice boomed against the white walls. "We don't want your pity."

Wendy turned to her. "I'm not offering any. I came here for Hakiam and Malikia—"

"I don't want her here. Tell her to go home," Leesa spoke over her.

"Oh, come on, Leesa. Will you quit it already?" Hakiam said.

Leesa pointed at Wendy. "She don't need to be here."

"My daughter came here out of concern for your child's well-being, young lady," Mr. Anderson said, stepping forward. "Let's stop the arguments. That's not what we came here for."

Hakiam watched as Leesa clamped her mouth shut. And then they waited.

Minutes passed, but they seemed more like hours.

Leesa stared at the wall and wrung her hands, then went to the snack machine.

Wendy kept telling Hakiam that everything would be all right.

A man rushed in cradling his seven- or eight-year-old son in his arms. The boy had his foot wrapped up in a white towel that had all but turned red.

Hakiam heard a moan from down the hall.

Leesa went down the hall to the bathroom, then came back.

Hakiam looked over at Wendy's father. He was trying to busy himself by going through his day planner and checking off items on his lists.

"I have news about Mal-i-kia," a bearded man in scrubs awkwardly sounded out as he walked into the dispute.

"I'm Malikia's mom. It's pronounced Ma-*leek*-i-a," Leesa corrected him.

"Never mind that," Wendy said, "how is she?"

"She's suffered a pretty good clunk to the head."

"We know that. Will she be all right?" Leesa said. Hakiam's heart pounded anew. The image of Malikia facedown in all the blood flooded his mind.

The man removed his glasses and said, "It looks like it. We're almost out of the woods, but she's gonna have to stay here tonight and into tomorrow for treatment and evaluation."

35

A few moments later, Wendy and her father walked quickly back to her car.

She put the key in the ignition. Her eyelashes glistened as tears flowed down her cheeks.

Wendy drove home, I-76. The silence intensified.

When they reached the house, her dad complained about the late hour and said at least it wasn't a school night. Then he went upstairs to the washroom to prepare himself for bed.

Wendy went to her room but stopped outside her door. Then she turned and entered the bathroom.

Her dad's face was wet.

Without acknowledging her, he walked past his daughter into his bedroom and shut the door.

He didn't usually ignore her like that. Wendy wondered if this was truly the end. Maybe she and her dad had grown too far apart. Maybe the politics of the world, the very black and white and gray, had intruded too deeply into their lives and now they had nothing to say to each other.

Wendy went back down the hallway and got into her bed. She thought about Malikia. Nothing was more out of order than a baby in a hospital. Wendy wondered how many Malikias there were in Misericordia Hospital. She wondered how many there were in Philadelphia. She wondered how many died and how many got better.

36

Before they left the hospital, Hakiam and Leesa were questioned for the better part of an hour.

"You were having a party."

Leesa shook her head violently. "It wasn't no party. Some people were just over."

"Who was watching the little girl?"

"Wasn't nobody watching her. She was sound asleep."

The woman in the pantsuit who had been taking notes exchanged a glance with Hakiam. He wondered what all this was leading to. What did this lady want and who at the hospital had called her?

His eyes moved to the bare walls, painted a glossy white to ward off stains. He heard another pair of footsteps coming down the hallway.

Before long, another lady came in. This one was in a blouse and skirt. She said she was from the Department of Human Services and started off by claiming she was "here to help."

The next thing Hakiam knew, other people were coming in with more questions. Men with suits and shiny shoes.

"How did she fall?"

Leesa's mouth twisted before she said, "She don't fall, she rolled."

"Haven't you heard of guardrails?"

"That costs money, which I don't have," Leesa said.

"Is this the time for a lecture?"

"Certain things are *normal* in a child's life, Miss Powell. The common cold, ear infections . . . but falling off a bed in one room while you carry on at a party in the next room is not."

"It was an accident!" Leesa said, pounding her fist on the table.

"Either way. X-rays are dangerous on someone that young," the woman said.

Leesa turned away.

"What do *you* have to say?" one of the social workers asked Hakiam.

Hakiam kept his chin up and looked past them to a place on the white wall on the other side of the room. "It was an accident. She just fell."

After more note-taking on their part, they left.

Leesa punched Hakiam on the arm. "You didn't sound very convincing."

"I told them it wasn't on purpose. What else do you want me to say?"

"Just don't say anything. Keep your mouth shut!"

Hakiam absorbed her anger and thought, *This is nothing. Malikia is the one really going through it.* He imagined how it must have felt crashing to the floor.

37

The next day was Sunday, which meant a fatter newspaper for Mr. Anderson, and he could take his time with breakfast. He usually had granola cereal with dates. Wendy knew his movements inside and out, and despite all the strife of the previous night, nothing had changed.

He spent the rest of the morning fiddling with white eyelet curtains. The fact that they were summer sheer, and here it was late November, was the reason he had finally found them at a price he was willing to pay, Wendy guessed.

She stood behind him for a long time without him turning around. It was like a comedy routine watching him try to hang them all by himself. The bay windows in the living room gave him quite a time.

"Well, are you going to stand there all day or are you going to help your father out?"

Wendy shifted positions and told him, "I'll just stand here."

He had his back to her, which made it easier to say that, but of course it was a joke. Or rather a dig. She grabbed a rod and inched the fabric onto it. He took the other end, and together they finished the front side of the house.

As they went to work on the south entrance, carrying the stepladder and the rest of the curtains, Wendy sighed and told him, "Thanks for coming with me to the hospital last night."

He didn't say anything. They began working side by side, and her dad suddenly spoke as if he were reading from a fortune cookie: "Sons aren't forever, but daughters are supposed to be."

"I'll always be your daughter, Dad," Wendy said, climbing up the ladder. Then she added under her breath, "Unfortunately."

As they finished up, her dad made a big deal about how Wendy had left an empty bag on the floor and what was the use of redecorating with an eyesore like that lying around.

At that point, Wendy thought, *So much for turning over a new leaf with all this impromptu father-daughter bonding.*

"See you later, Dad," she said, and headed for the stairs.

"Wendy," he called to her.

Now what? she wondered.

He spoke in a quiet voice, but it was his voice all the same. "When you get a status update about the baby, let me know."

38

The bedspread was twisted around Leesa, who was in a deep sleep. It was one hour past noon. She had pressed the back of her hand over her eyes to block out the sun.

Hakiam couldn't sleep. They had just gotten back from the hospital and he couldn't even sit still. He had to walk. He had to pace and pace. And when he did sit down, Leesa's cell was next to his wrist on the table.

Two people from the party last night had come back over: the girl in a tube top who had been passing food, and another girl who had been in a halter top. They looked beat, but it was probably more from the partying than the worry. They weren't just pretending to look at TV; they were watching it.

Around three in the afternoon, Leesa emerged from her bedroom. She didn't look particularly lost or found; she just joined them on the couch.

Hakiam looked at his cousin with disappointment,

then disgust. Since last night, something had shifted in him. He finally got it.

He went out into the hall to make more worry rounds.

When he came back in, his belongings were piled by the door in a paper shopping bag.

"What the hell is this?" he asked.

"What does it look like?" Leesa said.

"Your daughter could have died last night."

"Yeah, but she didn't. She's fine. The doctor just called while you were out."

"She's fine? She's conscious and everything?"

Leesa let out an exasperated sigh. "She's conscious and everything."

"Well, ain't you gonna go pick her up?"

"My mom's gonna. She's taking her in."

"So she's not even gonna live here? *That's* why I'm getting the shove out the door. You are a goddamn bitch, you know that?"

The girl in the tube top said, "Hey, man, we're trying to watch the show."

"Shut up, you, and mind your business."

He turned back to his cousin and looked her dead in the eye.

"You gonna just do me like this? I was nice to your daughter. I never meant you any harm."

Leesa didn't blink once as she told him, "Tell the truth for five seconds—you came here for a free lunch. You wanted it all to go your way. You wanted it all to be easy."

She walked over to the door and opened it.

"You bagged my shit on up to tell me to get out of

164

here? Leesa, you're really gonna do me like this? After I watched your kid for free?"

"Yeah, and she landed in the hospital, so thanks a lot."

Hakiam looked from his belongings to his cousin, then back to the paper sack. He grabbed his things and told her, "It's been real."

39

Wendy answered on the first ring.

"Where are you calling from? The hospital?" she asked.

"No, I got put out on the street."

"Don't tell me Leesa is still blaming you."

"Who else would she blame?"

"How is Malikia?" she asked.

"She woke up."

"Good. Is she able to have visitors yet?"

"I don't know. She's going to stay with my aunt for a while."

"Your aunt who's into church?"

"Yep."

"Well, that could be the answer. See if she'll take you in too."

"I don't know, maybe I'll start my job search again. Maybe I'll get lucky this time."

"You can't live at your job. Where will you sleep?" she asked him. Her own mind was searching for an answer. He could try a temporary shelter—but would he want to get mixed up with the system again? With social workers and counselors and the database entries? Hakiam needed a family, not a program.

Meanwhile, Hakiam said nothing. It felt like one of those awkward pauses they'd had when they first met.

"I'm just glad Malikia will be all right," he finally said.

Wendy nodded. "You know, when they say kids have hard heads, they're not kidding, Hakiam. Those skull bones don't join together till later in life. Sometimes falls aren't as bad as you think."

"Wendy, I can count on one hand the number of people in my life who give a damn. Thanks for coming when I called you. Thanks for giving a shit about Malikia."

A tear came to her eye and she quickly blinked it away.

"I'll always give a shit about Malikia, Hakiam. I'll always give a shit about you, too."

"I guess I'll see you at the center, Wendy."

"The center?" she asked incredulously.

"Yeah, you know, the place you volunteer at."

Her voice rose. "You're homeless and you have no source of income."

"Yeah," he said.

"What are you going to do? You can't stay on the

street." That was the last thing she was able to transmit to him before his quarter on the pay phone ran out.

The line went dead. Her mind buzzed with more questions. Where was he? What was he going to do with very little money and no place to live? Would she ever see him again?

40

Somewhere in the back of his mind he always knew
he'd end up in a hobo jungle. Where else did people
who didn't have a net end up? When they fell, they hit
the pavement.

It was sort of like that movie with Will Smith and
his son. Hakiam could now look forward to spending
the night in a toilet stall, but would there be a light
at the end of the tunnel, like in that flick? Would
he get a six-figure corporate job? Or an Oscar nomi-
nation?

Hakiam left Leesa's hood and its police sirens and
ambulance cries, its basketballs bouncing and children
screaming and doors opening and closing. He headed
for downtown, because why be homeless around a bunch
of poor people?

He hopped a turnstile and snuck onto an elevated
train. He rode to the end of the line, which was

downtown, then switched to another line. His goals were to stay warm and to stay out of the elements.

For a minute or two, he wished for seventy-five bucks. If he had that, he could catch a Greyhound bus back to Cincinnati and start all over again. Again.

After the third merry-go-round on the train, he had to stretch his legs. They felt thick and his butt was numb. He had to get out and move.

He got out at Sixteenth.

Rain fell heavy and fast from the sky. The street was washing out; the sky had opened. From the newsstand, he took a free Metro newspaper and put it over his head. It was soaked limp within moments. He was still hungry.

Down the street, a hotel doorman was gesturing to him.

Hakiam put his hand to his chest, asking, "You want me?"

The man kept waving.

Hakiam stepped closer to him. "What did you say?" he asked the man in coat and tails.

The doorman told him, "You need an umbrella."

Now he was wet, hungry, and broke. Night had fallen, and the hour he'd spent walking aimlessly in the rain hadn't helped at all.

He would have loved to have anything to eat. A sandwich—didn't matter what was stuck in the middle. Turkey. Baloney. A swipe of peanut butter.

A slice of cheese, even.

Libraries closed at eight. Stores in the city closed at

ten, but they hustled everyone out by nine-forty-five. And this being Sunday, they closed even earlier.

So he walked some more. Taxicabs and buses passed him.

The neon signs flashed. He'd never noticed how many tall buildings Philly had till then.

He ended up in a twenty-four-hour laundry.

He got a hot cup of coffee from the vending machine for twenty-five cents. He put in three more quarters and got a danish wrapped in plastic.

It was hard to bite into.

Hakiam noticed her the minute she walked in, a girl with a splash of blond hair and twinkling green eyes. She was the kind of girl he always had his eyes peeled for back in the day.

She put a load in the wash and took a seat near him on the bench, placing her handbag at her feet.

She had an iPod in her ears and her laptop was absorbing her attention. All he had to do was the old bump-and-swoop. He bet she had a few fives, maybe even a few twenties in her purse.

Hakiam thought about it and thought about it. It was almost like God (or some other all-seeing being who knew Hakiam was desperate) had sent her here to solve his problems.

All he had to do was reach out and take it.

But he couldn't get his body to cooperate. Temporary paralysis took over, and when he recovered, all he could do was tap her shoulder.

She took out her earplugs and turned to him with a warm smile.

"Your bag's on the floor."

"Oh," she said, like it was the farthest thing from her mind. "Thank you."

His smirk morphed into a smile back at her.

41

Wendy emptied her head during a history exam, traded ideas in her English literature peer group, and wrote a theorem on the board when her name was called in calculus. Thanks to a crazy global-warming day, she was spending lunch with Erin out on the school's rolling lawn.

"I've fallen out of bed before. I even fell out of a bunk bed—the top I bunk," Erin said.

"I'm sure you weren't an infant at the time."

"It's a shame." Erin nodded, shading her eyes from the sun. "So your dad really let Leesa have it."

"It wasn't very productive. He was just venting at her and Hakiam."

"Why Hakiam? He sounds like the hero in all this."

Wendy frowned and put things concisely: "It's guilt by association."

"Uh-oh. So, where does that leave you and Hakiam?"

"I don't know. I don't even know where he is. Leesa

173

kicked him out of her apartment. That just puts a nice little cherry on top of the sundae," Wendy said, listlessly spooning through her yogurt and granola.

Erin's eyebrows knitted together as she stilled her friend's hands. "Kyle and I had a blast that night. I hope we can all hang out again. Be sure to tell him that when you see him."

At the end of the school day, Wendy stopped by the Lower Merion post office. When she got up to the window, she found out that the application she was sending weighed a whopping one pound, five ounces.

"Howard, eh?" the bespectacled man behind the counter asked, reading the address.

"Yes," Wendy answered.

"I hope you get in," he said with a bright smile. "How would you like to send this?"

"Express, please."

42

Hakiam had stayed up all night. The sun rising in the morning, with birds flying through the trees, wasn't necessarily the most beautiful sight to him. But at least he had a few things scheduled.

He went to the downtown mall between Eighth and Tenth and took the escalator to the ground floor, where the food court was. Mickey D's stood there, shining like a yellow and red beacon, exuding the smell of coffee and Egg McMuffins and hash browns.

He entered the store and stood off to the side till the manager noticed him. The moonfaced woman asked, "May I help you?"

"I need a job, like now," he told her.

"Right this minute?"

"Yep."

"Did you fill out an application?"

"Not here, but a few weeks ago I went up and down Chestnut Street. I ain't heard nothing."

"But you didn't apply here?"

"Look," Hakiam said, "I—I want a job. I do. I know this ain't the right way to go about things but I'm nearly out of money, so if you need someone to do whatever you do here, I'll do it. Cuz I'm almost out of money."

He could tell the woman was trying hard to keep her jaw from dropping open. Finally, she gave him a half smile and said, "Well, we could always use a hand."

After giving him paperwork that she said he could fill out during his lunch break, she showed him to the mop closet, where the rags and disinfectants were stored. His first task was to wipe down the tables from the breakfast rush.

As he trudged his way through the paces of his new job, cleaning off crumbs and spilled orange juice, he spent the first hour in a state of shock. It was unbelievable to him that he'd actually been hired. All he did was ask!

He looked at the patrons. They didn't really look back; there was no real connection. His role relegated him to being the proverbial fly on the wall, and that was fine with him. Hakiam moved on to putting the straws in the dispensers and the wad of napkins into the canisters, and before he knew it, it was time to punch out.

He was one for one. He decided to press his luck.

He caught a bus heading west and got out near Catharine Street.

He walked quickly on the cold streets, passing morose faces, church spires, and leafless trees.

After he made it to her address, he paused before ringing the bell. He took a deep breath.

The door opened.

"Hakiam, Hakiam, it's been so long, too long. I had a feeling you'd be coming by. Every lost sheep comes back into the fold. I've been praying about it," she said, and held her arms out.

"I didn't even get a chance to ring—"

"I saw you clear down the block."

Hakiam accepted her tight hug. She was a thin woman, covered up in a long-sleeved shirt and a skirt to her ankles. Her Afro was gathered in a headband.

She started to say her signature line: "God is great—"

"All the time," Hakiam finished for her.

"I'm glad you came. Let me get you something to eat—"

"Don't go to the trouble."

"It's no trouble, Hakiam. I'm happy to do it." She left the hall and went into the kitchen. Hakiam followed and steadied her hand before she was able to reach for anything on the shelf.

"I just wanted to see Malikia," he told her.

She nodded and led him upstairs to Malikia's bedroom. "She's been asleep for most of the afternoon. The doctor said that's good."

Hakiam's heart started pounding hard. Aunt Josephine had the crib set up in the center of the room. Beside that she had a rocking chair with a Bible placed on the armrest. It was open to Matthew, chapter 18.

Aunt Josephine took the book in her hands. She began reading with passion in her voice. "'Whoever therefore humbles himself as this little child, the same is

177

the greatest in the Kingdom of Heaven. Whoever receives one such little child in my name receives me . . . '"

Hakiam swallowed hard and his eyes glazed over. This was what had driven him to avoid his aunt since he'd come to Philly. He had a low threshold for all this born-again stuff.

Malikia gave a random kick.

"'But,'"Aunt Josephine continued with the quotation, "'whoever causes one of these little ones who believe in me to stumble, it would be better for him that a huge millstone should be hung around his neck, and that he should be sunk in the depths of the sea.'"

Hakiam's eyes panned the rest of the room and stopped on a teddy bear that was on the nightstand. It was holding a single yellow rose.

Aunt Josephine pointed. "That's from that nice-looking girl who came by yesterday afternoon. She said she knew Malikia through you. She said her name was—"

"Wendy."

Malikia began to stir again.

"Is it okay to pick her up?" Hakiam asked.

His aunt nodded.

Hakiam walked over to the wooden crib and let down the gate. Malikia looked small and lost in the crisp white bedding. There were bandages over her head. The rest of her was swaddled, so he couldn't tell if she had any more bandaging. She was very still but breathing steadily.

"Why don't you stay here," his aunt said, moving in beside him. She gently patted Malikia. "You can stay with me if you want. Leesa was by. She told me about the party and how you found Malikia. I told her not to blame you. I told her you saved her life. You did a good thing, Hakiam."

"I'm just glad she's going to be all right."

At that very moment, Malikia burst into tears.

Hakiam sighed and said, "Well, baby, I guess you're stuck with me again."

43

Wendy was all dressed up in her favorite outfit: willow green roll-neck wool sweater, a long skirt with microdots, and low leather boots. She waved hello to Mr. Clayton, the guard, who was busy eating hot wings.

She hustled up the stairs to the center and saw a miraculous thing. The book was cracked open, and Hakiam was reading.

He looked up at her and they exchanged a deeper gaze.

She hooked her tote bag around the chair.

Late-afternoon sunlight illuminated the room.

"Well," she said, sliding into the seat directly across from his. "We might as well get started."

About the Author

A Philadelphia native and a Virgo, Allison Whittenberg studied dance for years before switching her focus to writing. She has a master's degree in English from the University of Wisconsin. Her middle-grade novels about Charmaine Upshaw, *Sweet Thang* and *Hollywood and Maine,* are available from Yearling Books and Delacorte Press, respectively, and her first novel for teen readers, *Life Is Fine,* is available from Delacorte Press. Allison enjoys traveling, and she loves to hear from her readers. Visit her online at www.allisonwhittenberg.com.